TO
COMFORT
A
KING

TO
COMFORT
A
KING

A NOVEL

DEBBIE GILLILAND

AMBASSADOR INTERNATIONAL
GREENVILLE, SOUTH CAROLINA & BELFAST, NORTHERN IRELAND

www.ambassador-international.com

To Comfort A King

ISBN: 978-1-62020-274-6
eISBN: 978-1-62020-376-7

Typesetting: Joshua Frederick
E-book conversion: Anna Riebe

AMBASSADOR INTERNATIONAL
Emerald House
427 Wade Hampton Blvd.
Greenville, SC 29609, USA
www.ambassador-international.com

AMBASSADOR BOOKS
The Mount
2 Woodstock Link
Belfast, BT6 8DD, Northern Ireland, UK
www.ambassadormedia.co.uk

The colophon is a trademark of Ambassador

In Memory of

My Mentor and Friend

Merlin Wilkins

1928-2012

"When King David was old and well advanced in years, he could not keep warm even when they put covers over him. So his servants said to him, 'Let us look for a young virgin to attend the king and take care of him. She can lie beside him so that our lord the king may keep warm.'

"Then they searched throughout Israel for a beautiful girl and found Abishag, a Shunamite, and brought her to the king. The girl was very beautiful; she took care of the king and waited on him."

I Kings 1:1-4 (NIV)

CHAPTER 1

ABISHAG STOOD SILENTLY BEFORE THE doors to the king's private chambers, a veil of resignation draped across her countenance. There was none of the trembling anticipation other maidens surely would have felt when summoned by the king. Her king was old, and dying; and though she had been chosen because of her beauty, she had been commissioned simply to keep the king warm.

The huge doors opened. The king's servants bowed as the queen led the way to the royal bed. Abishag followed Bathsheba's quick steps, trailing the sweet scent of the queen's perfumes on her flowing robes. How peculiar it seemed for her introduction to the king to be at the hand of his favorite wife.

The king's bed was elevated from the level of any who appeared before him in his private chambers. Massive posts heavily carved with ornate flare rose from each corner of the bed. A thick tapestry of dark greens and purples was draped at the head, while fine satin lengths of pure white swagged between the other posts. A heavy woolen spread dyed to royal purple covered the king. Several cushions propped him almost to a sitting position.

With a flick of her hand, Bathsheba dismissed the servant at the king's bedside. She stepped up quietly and sat down next to the silent form. For a moment, her eyes took measure of the king's condition. Even as he slept, cold tremors shook his body. Bathsheba rested a warm palm against his cheek, and only then did he open his eyes. The woman combed her fingers through his white hair, and she leaned to kiss his dry lips.

"I have brought Abishag, my lord," Bathsheba whispered.

The king looked up at her wearily, as if he were an unwilling participant in this introduction. He closed his eyes and in the darkness found the strength to address the young woman. "Come closer, child."

Abishag had remained at a distance, watching the king and queen with a sense of intrusion. The king's faint voice prodded her with the reality of her presence before the king of Israel. She bowed as she had been instructed and approached the bedside with lowered eyes. Bathsheba rose and stood to face her.

For an eternal moment, the king was silent. Abishag had not yet been granted permission to look upon him, but she imagined his eyes inspecting her, this young woman who had been chosen from all Israel to care for him.

"She is indeed very beautiful, Bathsheba. But what have I to do with beauty at my age?"

Bathsheba offered her hand to Abishag and drew her closer to the king. "She plays the harp, my lord."

"Does she?" he said with renewed strength. "Have her play for me now."

Bathsheba motioned to the harp at the foot of the bed.

Abishag stepped down and sat beside the king's gilded harp. She touched its smoothness with awed fingers. She had never seen such a magnificent instrument. The thought of strumming its strings delighted her. She lifted the harp to her lap and gently smoothed her palm across the strings. At last, she pulled one string and then another. Her soul escaped to a familiar retreat, and she played the quiet lullaby that had so often comforted her own dying mother.

When her fingers paused, the king whispered, "Well done, child. There might be a good use for you after all." His words voiced his conviction that her commissioned services were unnecessary.

Abishag carefully settled the harp back in place and stood. "Thank you, my king. If it pleases you, I shall play often."

"It will occupy your time here, at any rate," he muttered.

Bathsheba sat beside him again and stroked his face. "She will please you in many ways, my lord. Wait and see."

"It pleases me most to have *you* here," the king argued.

"I shall come every day," Bathsheba promised. "But Abishag has young and soft hands to rub warmth into your bones. As you enjoy her beauty, she will remind you of our youthful passion."

"I have not forgotten," the king countered. A weary smile crept across his lips.

"I must leave you now," Bathsheba said softly. "Abishag will stay. Whatever you need, she will assist you." Again she bent to kiss the king. When she stood, her gaze fastened on the tired face of the king. Even a stranger in the palace could not have missed the bond between the king and his queen.

"Tend my lord carefully," she admonished Abishag as she turned to leave. Behind her, the chamber doors closed quietly.

CHAPTER 2

One week earlier . . .

"HAVE I NO VOICE IN this matter, Father?" Abishag asked.

Eliezer busied himself tying on his outer robe for the cool day, but the question hung in the silence between them. He paused and considered his eldest daughter as she waited for his response. How could a child of his be so beautiful? Coal-black hair glistened in the morning light. Abishag had pulled it to a tight knot at the base of her neck to restrain it during her day's work about the house; but when it flowed freely, silken curls bounced against her shoulders. A slender nose scooped down to meet her full lips. The soft cheeks he had so often cupped with his roughened hands glowed in golden perfection. Eyes the color of aged honey looked back at him, piercing his confidence that he had made the right decision.

"It will only be for a short time, Daughter," he said at last. "It is reported that King David is near death. You will keep him comfortable in his last days, and then you will return home to us."

"But why have I been chosen for this?" Abishag questioned.

Eliezer had wondered that for several days, but he dared not question his good fortune. Abishag's commission had fetched him a considerable price, though he cringed at the thought of accepting it. "Your special way of helping the ill must have been reported to the king's ministers," he said. "People watch you. They see how your gentle hands soften death's harshness. They have heard how your sweet music comforts an aching body. And . . ." Her father paused, not certain he wished to admit to Abishag's greatest asset. "You are very beautiful."

"Beautiful?" Abishag repeated incredulously. "What has *that* to do with comforting an old, dying king?"

"I do not know, Daughter." He sighed. In truth, Eliezer had avoided the answer to that question. Maidens who were invited to the king's chambers did not return home. Accepting this fate for his eldest daughter had been difficult.

"What is to become of Jezreel and Nathan?" Abishag demanded.

"Jezreel is growing up, my child. Why, she is only three years younger than you. She has watched you, and she will quickly learn to care for your responsibilities. And Nathan? He is just a child. He will become accustomed to your absence."

"But they have just lost their mother!" Abishag exclaimed, daring to mention the death that had recently devastated their family.

There was no need to remind Eliezer. His grief had transformed from the exhausted acceptance of his wife's death into a bitter anger that he had been robbed so early of his dearest friend. Loneliness now clung to him like a menacing shadow.

"I will do my best, Abishag," he replied.

"I know, Father," Abishag whispered. "I just do not know if I can bear to leave my family. And what of Joseph? Has he been told?"

Eliezer's shoulders stiffened at the mention of Joseph. Abishag had been promised to him for several years. Had it not been for her mother's illness, Abishag would have been married by now.

Kings and queens did not concern themselves with obligations of ordinary people. If the palace ministers desired Abishag's services, no amount of bartering would excuse her.

"I have spoken to Joseph's father," Eliezer answered. "The whole village knows of it anyway. I think some may have known before I did."

It was true. News traveled through the fish market faster than flies. If it were remarkable news, it was foisted about with even greater urgency. And the news that Abishag, daughter of Eliezer, had been summoned to the palace was remarkable news indeed!

"When am I to go, Father?" Abishag asked quietly.

"In a week," he answered as he turned to leave for his stall at the market.

Abishag stood in the doorway and watched her father disappear down the street. His was a melancholy walk, slow steps reluctant to reach the day's work. There he would be obliged to pleasantly greet his customers and make idle conversation with them. He had manned his fish stall for many years, and most of the patrons were aware of his wife's death. Thinking their few days of spoken condolences were the extent of their obligation to him, they had forgotten his loss. Still, the sorrow always shadowed his countenance.

When her father walked out of sight, Abishag turned back to her fire. She had not heard Jezreel enter the room. Abishag found frightened eyes fixed on her. Jezreel's eyes quivered with a sad understanding of a conversation her deaf ears could not have heard between her father and her sister.

Abishag opened her arms, and Jezreel rushed to embrace her. Her curly head pressed close against Abishag's heart. It seemed the child grew an inch between each morning's greetings. Her father was right. Jezreel was becoming a young woman right before their eyes. The delight that once sparkled in her eyes with the slightest of life's ecstasies had faded into a dull acceptance that there was more to life than childish pleasures.

Abishag tenderly tilted the child's chin to speak to her eyes. "Little Jezreel," Abishag whispered, "I will not be gone for long." *King David is an old man,* she reasoned to herself, *and he is ill. Even my magical touch cannot keep him alive forever.*

Jezreel tightened her arms around her sister's waist as if to prevent her leaving. Abishag rested her palm against the girl's mussed hair for a moment, and then her fingers began to work through the tangles left from the night's sleep. The black curls stretched out in her fingers and bounced back into ornery disarray. Jezreel mirrored the very image of their mother. If the perfectly arched eyebrows and the slender nose did not tell, one look at Jezreel's eyes could catch off guard any who had known her mother and send a little gasp of recognition through his heart.

How cruel it seemed to Abishag that their God would flaw this perfection with ears that could not hear. Was it crueler that He had allowed young Jezreel to know for a time the chatter of birds, the gentle thump of rain upon the roof, and the harmony of her parents' laughter? Now, even the harshest clap of thunder could not shake the interminable silence that enveloped her. Would it have been better for Jezreel to never know those sounds? Abishag had questioned God about this ever since the fever had robbed Jezreel of her hearing.

Nevertheless, Jezreel did hear with her eyes. Abishag was certain her little sister had understood her promise that she would not be gone for long, and she would wrap her arms around that hope in Abishag's absence.

Abishag took hold of Jezreel's shoulders and gently pushed her away, so their eyes could meet. "It's time to wake your lazy brother."

Jezreel's hesitant smile curled into a quiet giggle as they set out for Nathan's couch.

The early morning sun pushed through the window and nudged Nathan to a reluctant wakefulness. He covered his eyes with his pillow. Abishag smiled. She knew he was pretending it was still dark, and that his sleep could go on forever. It was Friday. There would be extra chores for him today in preparation for the Sabbath. He would grumble at the inequity of a young boy being burdened with so many responsibilities. Abishag would ignore him—for a while—but there was a limit to even Abishag's patience.

But the game was just beginning. Nathan hid under his covers for a little longer. Abishag watched and waited. Her little brother was at that awkward age—too old to enjoy the carefree abandon of a toddler, but too young to make much contribution to the daily tasks in a household. Still, there were jobs for him to do, and Abishag would see that he did not forget.

Abishag and Jezreel approached Nathan's cot on tiptoe, without alerting the little boy, whose head was still covered with his pillow. At once they fell down on his couch and tickled him until he begged for mercy. His pillow tumbled to the floor, and the sun kissed his golden cheeks. In the brightness, he squinted and pulled the covers over his head.

"It is time to be up," Abishag scolded. She patted the black curls that peeked out and drew the covers down past Nathan's chin. Long, thick eyelashes squeezed together as he pushed back the sunshine again. Finally, he opened his eyes to greet the day.

What beautiful eyes this child has, Abishag thought. Just now they sparkled with mischief; but not so long ago, they reflected the sorrow he found in the faces of his family. A child so young could not fully comprehend death's permanent separation from his mother, but he saw their anguish and it became his own. One day, though, his eyes would learn to maneuver hearts, and pleasures would be granted him solely for their sake.

CHAPTER 3

ABISHAG STARTED OUT FOR THE meat market, leaving Jezreel scrubbing vegetables and Nathan hauling kindling for the oven. Both chores would be completed before she returned. Jezreel would look for another, but Nathan would escape. In another year, he would be old enough to spend the days with his father at the fish market. There were little things he could do there to help, and he would gradually learn the business. For now, however, Nathan was still a child. Abishag smiled as she imagined him sneaking off to find his friends.

The crisp air chilled her cheeks. Abishag pulled the shawl closer. *Only a week before I leave home,* she thought. *And how long before I return?* Her father promised it would be a short time, even as she had promised Jezreel. Abishag had attended illness and death enough times to know that often the end came at the price of extended misery. Better that she not count on being home too soon.

Abishag looked about with a new awareness that she would not walk these streets again for a while. She nodded to neighbors she would not see again. She breathed in the smell of her village, convinced that it would not be quite the same when she returned. Or was it she herself who would not be quite the same? There was a comfortable familiarity with her village. She would abandon that comfort when she passed through the gates of the palace.

The palace, indeed! There were parts of her own village she had never visited. She had never found a reason to go beyond her village boundaries. What little she knew of Jerusalem was market hearsay her father chose to share. The fishermen who stocked Eliezer's stall made deliveries in Jerusalem, and they delivered both news and gossip with their goods.

Joseph had been to Jerusalem, though. He and his father made trips to the city to deliver completed orders for furniture. It delighted Abishag to listen to the accounts Joseph brought back—people he had seen, things he had heard, places he had been. He seemed to step easily between the extremities of Shunem and Jerusalem, but he vowed he would never live in the city. Life seemed less precious there.

There! Joseph had finally surfaced in her thoughts. Father had told her that Joseph knew she had been summoned to the palace. He did not tell her, however, how Joseph had accepted news that would affect his own life as well as Abishag's. Eliezer no doubt wanted to believe his daughter's absence would be short. Joseph could and would just have to wait for Abishag to return.

It seemed to Abishag that Joseph had already waited for her. Their families had been planning the ceremony before her mother's illness struck. Now, many of the young women Abishag's age made the daily trip to the market toting babies on their hips. Abishag had tried to imagine caring for a husband and a child. It could not be much different from caring for her father and Jezreel and Nathan. Mostly, it was exhausting work. Sometimes she wondered how it would feel for Joseph to hold her close. Surely that part of marriage must be an awesome thing!

"Abishag! There you are." The man from her thoughts materialized before her eyes. "Your father told me you would be coming to the market."

Joseph's broad smile chased away Abishag's fears that he did not care enough for her to wait for her return from the palace assignment. Abishag looked at him with the same sense of impending separation as she looked at her village. She sketched in her memory his delighted face, noting the lines that pleated the corners of his eyes when he smiled at her. He kept his beard short. In the sunlight, a hint of red chased through his hair and into his beard.

Joseph took the market basket from Abishag's arm and dropped it to the ground. He reached out both hands and embraced her hands in his. His palms were toughened from the grip of hammers and planes and chisels.

"I wanted to see you before you leave," he said.

"Father would have you come for a meal," Abishag replied. "I was going to speak to him about it tonight."

"We can still do that," Joseph answered with a smile. "But I have something to show you. Something I want you to see before you leave." His enthusiasm was childlike and contagious.

"What is it?" Abishag asked eagerly.

Abishag's curiosity drew a smile across Joseph's face. "It is a surprise. Follow me." He kept one hand around hers and turned away from the market.

Abishag pulled against him until he stopped and turned back to face her. "The children are at home," she said. "They will wonder what has become of me."

"We will go by and let them know you are with me," Joseph answered.

"But I have not been to the market yet," she reminded him.

Disappointment crept across Joseph's face. "Of course." He sighed. "Make your purchases, and then I will show you my surprise." He sat on a step in the courtyard to wait for Abishag's return.

Eliezer could bring fish home any day she requested it, so Abishag did not take the time to stop at his stall. She wondered if Joseph had shared his secret with her father, as a man might, and she did not want to allow the opportunity to hear about it from anyone but Joseph. She headed to Reuben's fruit stall and selected oranges and apples and a heavy cluster of grapes.

At Zebulon's vegetable stall Abishag chose carrots and onions. Old Zebulon watched her carefully as she placed the vegetables in her basket. He had obviously heard the news. Abishag could guess exactly what the old man was thinking: *What a tragedy for a young woman like Abishag to be assigned to the care of a dying old man. Even if he was the king!*

"We will see you again soon," he encouraged as he took the coins from Abishag's hand. A timid smile acknowledged his kindness.

At the meat stall, Abishag quickly chose a slab of mutton, mentally calculating how she would prepare the meat. There would be roasted mutton for one day and mutton stew for another.

Finally, Abishag hurried to meet Joseph. He had been watching for her and started toward her. He took the heavy basket from her arm.

"I hope I did not rush you," he said. His enthusiasm had not mellowed with the delay. He walked so quickly that Abishag's steps scurried to keep up. Joseph was a full head taller than Abishag, and it seemed his strides could cover twice the distance of hers.

A long silence rested between them as they walked toward Eliezer's home. Strangely, Joseph did not mention her leaving. Abishag longed to hear his reassurance that her absence would change nothing between them. Surely he understood that it was not her choice to go!

Jezreel was just returning from the well when Abishag and Joseph arrived. Keeping household water supplied was a responsibility that would fall upon Jezreel now. Joseph hurried to help Jezreel set down the heavy pot. Jezreel tipped her head to thank him. He was no stranger in their home, but Jezreel still hesitated to look into his eyes. Abishag excused her sister's reticence, thinking she nurtured some imagination that Joseph was replacing her in Abishag's heart. How could she explain to Jezreel that there are little niches in one's heart that different people must fill? Abishag was only beginning to understand that herself.

She moved close to Jezreel and addressed her eyes. "Joseph wants to show me something. I will be back shortly." Jezreel nodded and watched Joseph take Abishag's hand as they turned to leave.

"Where are you taking me?" Abishag dared to ask.

"It's not far," Joseph said with a wide grin. "Come on!"

They had walked only a short distance when Joseph stopped and motioned Abishag to turn off the street. They stood at the entrance to a small home. The windows were shut up tightly, even so late in the morning. The sturdy door was not weathered enough to have been in place for long. It was very quiet.

Joseph watched her face intently. "It will be our home, Abishag. Yours and mine. We will raise our children here."

"Ours, Joseph? Really?" Her voice quivered with surprise.

"Are you pleased?" Joseph asked. "It is close to your father's home."

Abishag's mind wrestled with the words for her reply. This was the reassurance she had desired that things would not change between them while she was gone. This was also proof that Joseph understood her responsibility to her father. She would need to learn to listen for this man's affection in unusual places.

"It's perfect, Joseph!" she exclaimed.

CHAPTER 4

THE WEEK BEFORE SHE LEFT for the palace passed too quickly. Abishag spent late hours finishing the mending. She drilled Jezreel on how to tend the fire carefully. Together, they planned meals for several days. Abishag took Jezreel to the market and showed her how to get the best piece of meat, which was seldom the one offered first. They cleaned the rooms and beat the mats.

Exhausted, Abishag worked to pack a trunk with the things she would take to the palace. She folded her worn shifts and stacked them in the trunk. Two woven shawls added the only color to her wardrobe. Tucked into a little wooden box were her herbs for healing—a prized inheritance from her mother. There was cinnamon, sage, thyme, turmeric, ginger, rosemary, saffron, and basil stored in small compartments in the wooden box. A mortar and pestle nestled in a section made slightly larger than the other compartments.

Before she closed the lid to her trunk, Abishag padded her harp into place. She would not leave home without it. The harp had belonged to her mother. Abishag remembered sitting in the candlelight on cool evenings and listening to the sweet music that flowed from her mother's fingers. It had fascinated young Abishag how strings that looked so much alike could produce such different sounds. In time, her mother recognized Abishag's passion for music and began to teach her how to pull melodies from the strings.

Abishag did not have much to call her own. A single trunk contained it all. Her father had been told that the palace would provide her bedding and bathing necessities. Abishag imagined her simple clothing would be adequate for the servant's duties she would be assigned. It was not her intention to be noticed there.

On her last morning at home, Joseph lifted the trunk to the small cart he and his father used to haul completed carpentry orders. Nathan and Jezreel guarded the doorway so that Abishag could not leave without bidding them goodbye. Abishag had not imagined how much it would hurt to leave them. Abishag accepted Nathan's quick hug. *He must think I will return in only a day or two,* she thought. Nathan stepped aside and allowed Jezreel to take his place.

Abishag felt Jezreel's heart pounding as they embraced. The sisters' souls had grown together over the years. Separating without tearing their tender connections would be a delicate task. Abishag breathed in deeply the fresh smell of her sister's hair. She felt the reluctance in Jezreel's arms as they parted.

Abishag took her sister's hands in her own and spoke to her eyes. "Take care of Father and Nathan for me. I will miss you so much." Abishag knew that Jezreel's world was about to become a silent and lonely existence without her sister's companionship. That was the most difficult part of leaving.

It was a long, dusty ride to Jerusalem. Abishag pulled her woolen cloak close while the crisp fall air whipped her robe against her legs. Once they were inside the city gates, Abishag found much to take her mind off her discomfort. The crowded streets buzzed with the noise of animals and men. The homes squatted together so closely that they often shared a wall. It seemed there were beggars at every corner.

As they neared the palace, the homes they passed assumed a more prosperous aura. Their windows were draped with bright cloth, and most boasted a second level, topped with a patio. The people in these streets wore colorful robes and scurried about with a rush of importance.

"Out of the way!" a man shouted at Joseph and his cart. "Quick, now!"

Joseph pulled the cart over to one side and stopped. Moments later, a procession of horses pushed through the crowded street. At the lead was a pair of young men who shouted at each other and laughed loudly against the thundering hooves of their mounts.

"Will you tell your father what we have done today?" one asked.

"Even the king does not need to know everything," came the reply. They laughed again at the mischief they seemed to have committed. The noise of the tramping horses was deafening. The dirt they kicked up settled down heavily on those they left in their path.

"Who do you think that was?" Abishag asked Joseph as she coughed the dust out of her lungs.

"The one on the lead horse was Adonijah—one of King David's sons," Joseph answered.

"You *know* that man?" Abishag asked with a hint of disbelief in her words.

"Of course I don't *know* him," admitted Joseph. "But I have seen him ride through the city before, and I have heard people talk about him."

"He seemed very inconsiderate," Abishag assessed.

"He is royalty." Joseph spat. "They are not required to be considerate."

Abishag turned to look at him as she reviewed his contemptuous answer. She was going to live with royalty. Would they all be loud and pushy and inconsiderate? If the king's own son was haughty, what would the king be like?

When they arrived at the palace gate, footmen lifted Abishag's trunk from the cart. "The queen is expecting you," they advised. "Follow us." The brusque command allowed little time for farewells with her father and Joseph.

"Serve the king well, Daughter. When you return, you will have a fine wedding celebration." Eliezer's broad smile disguised his reluctance to give Abishag up to the palace. His rough hands embraced her shoulders awkwardly, and he kissed her on the forehead.

Joseph took her hands one last time. "You will be busy tending the king," he whispered. "I will stay busy building furniture for our home. Perhaps the time will pass quickly."

Abishag accepted his encouragement with a nod. Words she longed to say lodged in her throat. "Perhaps," she agreed. "I will look forward to seeing the fine things you will make." She needed to ask one last thing of Joseph. "Please keep your eyes on Jezreel," she whispered. "She will not ask for help."

Joseph nodded at the request. Agreeing to look after her might be the most important promise he could offer Abishag.

The footmen waited at the palace gate impatiently. Abishag dared not make them call to her a second time. She swallowed all the tender words she had for both men and turned her back to the only world she had ever known.

CHAPTER 5

BATHSHEBA'S SLIGHT FIGURE DOMINATED THE throne room. Word had been sent to her that Abishag had arrived. At last she would set eyes on this young woman whose reputation boasted such astounding perfection. It was Bathsheba who had insisted that the woman chosen should play the harp. That had been deemed a frivolous requirement, but Bathsheba knew her king well enough to understand that the music would do as much to comfort his soul as anything else. It was the ministers' qualifications that the woman be both beautiful and a virgin. Reports that a creature with such a combination of attributes had been found were a bit of a surprise to the queen.

Bathsheba heard footsteps approaching the throne room. She smoothed her robe and fingered the royal collar that glistened around her neck. She was the queen, the king's beloved wife, and the mother of his son who had been promised the crown. This Abishag threatened none of these honors, not even if she were the most beautiful woman in the kingdom!

The procession halted at the entrance to the throne room. "Your highness, we present Abishag, daughter of Eliezer, of Shunem." The room echoed with the attendant's introduction. "Bow to your queen," he whispered sharply to Abishag. It was obvious to all that the young woman had no instruction in court conduct.

Bathsheba watched in silent amusement as the sight of the throne room absorbed Abishag's attention. Magnificent carvings she herself had selected decorated the walls. Tapestries with rich colors draped the side walls in symmetrical spaces. A crimson carpet spanned the distance between her throne and the feet of Abishag. The throne itself was a carpentry masterpiece of inlaid woods, deep mahogany contrasting with light oak, all complemented by the red cedar. At last, Abishag's gaze climbed the three steps at the base of the throne, and their eyes locked upon each other's.

"Welcome, Abishag." Bathsheba's voice was soft and warm. Abishag had bowed, but she now raised her eyes and nodded to the queen. "Please come forward," the queen invited. "We have much to learn about each other."

The attendants remained at the entrance while Abishag moved to the foot of the throne. She bowed again, trembling with her inadequate preparation for this moment. She raised her face once again to meet her queen. "It is a great honor, your highness," the girl whispered.

"I am pleased to finally meet you, Abishag," the queen replied. "I have heard many remarkable things about you."

"I am not remarkable, your highness," Abishag countered softly.

"The king's ministers believe otherwise," Bathsheba answered. "Much has been reported to me of your way with comforting the ill. I have been told you play the harp." There was a long pause. "And anyone can see that the reports of your beauty were not exaggerated."

Abishag lowered her eyes. "My mother showed me how quiet words and gentle hands can soothe an aching body. She taught me how to pluck the strings of a harp to make happy music. And if I am beautiful, I'm sure it is because of my mother as well."

Bathsheba considered the girl's response. "Your mother is to be commended on all counts."

"My mother was a remarkable woman," Abishag whispered.

"You miss her very much, I see," the queen said tenderly.

"I do."

"Tell me about your family," Bathsheba asked.

Abishag looked again into the face of the queen. "My father is Eliezer. He has a fish stall at the market in Shunem. Jezreel, my sister, is three years younger than I. My brother, Nathan, is just a child."

Bathsheba noted the brevity of the introductions. She sensed there was much the girl was unwilling to share. In time, perhaps Abishag would allow her to become better acquainted with the people in her life.

"I trust it will not be too great a hardship for your family to manage without you," the queen offered.

"They will get along. Joseph will be there if they need anything."

"Joseph?" This man had not been mentioned before. It was obvious by the way Abishag said his name that he was someone important to her.

"Joseph and I were to be married, but my mother's illness delayed it," Abishag explained.

So, there is a man in Abishag's life, after all, the queen realized. It seemed impossible to Bathsheba that a young woman so beautiful as Abishag had not married. Would this Joseph complicate matters, or would he prove to keep Abishag's passion occupied while she attended to the king?

"And now the king further delays your marriage?" Bathsheba questioned.

Abishag's timid smile affirmed the queen's suggestion. "It is an honor for me to be asked to care for the king, your highness. I will do it to the best of my ability as long as it pleases him."

The quiet pledge hummed with sincerity. "You will please him, of that I am certain," Bathsheba remarked. "But first, we must get you settled in and ready to meet the king. My attendants will handle these matters for us."

At the mention of their services, the attendants fluttered to the queen's bidding. Abishag was ushered back into the great hallway and led past countless doors. At last, the attendants turned her into an entry and pushed the massive doors open to reveal a large room filled with the chatter of several women lounging on satin cushions. Abishag's simple brown robe suddenly seemed ridiculous among so many silken gowns. The room smelled of lavender and vanilla and heady spices Abishag could not identify.

The chatter froze into silence when Abishag entered. Some of the women stood to better view the visitor. Their eyes inspected Abishag with cool superiority. They did not seem surprised to see her, just surprised that she was so commonly attired. None spoke a word to her.

Heavy tapestry curtains separated an adjoining room. The warmth of steaming water could be felt even at a distance. The queen's attendants directed Abishag behind the curtains. "We have been directed to bathe you," they announced, reaching to pull the woolen robe from Abishag's shoulders.

"I beg your pardon, but I am capable of bathing myself," Abishag objected. She pulled her robe close to her and wrapped her arms together.

The attendants granted her a moment's hesitancy. "The queen instructed us to bathe you," one attendant repeated. "While you are in the palace, you will be waited upon for such things. It is the way things are done."

Abishag swallowed her pride and allowed her robe to be removed. The attendant tossed it aside beyond the pile of thick towels. Abishag's private soul longed to sink into the water and cover herself, but she stood motionless, staring at the wall opposite her. After the attendants had removed their sandals, they stepped into the water and held out their hands to assist Abishag down the wide step into the shallow water.

She was not invited to lower herself into the steaming water. Instead, the attendants poured cupfuls of water over her and soft sponges scrubbed against her skin. The hands were gentle but intolerant of her modesty. They lifted her arms and soaked the tender pits. They nudged beneath her breasts with the wet sponges. They forced her legs apart to cleanse her private places. At last, they reached for the heavy towels and gathered them around Abishag's trembling body. Abishag gratefully pulled the towels close.

The bathing process was not completed, however. The attendants took the towels from around her and directed her to lie down on a padded slab close to the water. Their warm hands began to spread perfumed oil over her body, massaging the flesh they touched. Soon the room's steam and the oil's sweet smell soothed Abishag into semi-consciousness; her body relaxed beneath the kneading hands. They combed through Abishag's long black curls until they hung freely around her shoulders. A pale robe of silky cloth was fitted to her and tied with a satin belt. The attendants gathered her hair up from her neck with pearl combs. Slippers of the softest leather were placed on her feet.

The attendants collected the damp towels and the soiled clothing. "You will take your noon meal here, and then the queen will call for you."

"If I may ask," Abishag whispered, "who are these women?"

"They are the king's concubines. But they have not been asked for in some time now." The attendant's voice was laced with sarcastic pleasure.

That said, she ushered Abishag out of the bathing room and returned to the waiting scrutiny of the other women. She was directed to an empty couch, where she stared beyond the knowing smiles of her new companions.

"Welcome to the harem," one voice called coolly.

"A harem of forgotten women," another voice muttered.

"Perhaps a new figure will revive our king's desire," one suggested.

Bitter laughter filled the room. The king was dying, and not even a beautiful virgin like this one would be able to fan the embers of his passion.

Abishag grew angry at the taunts. "I am here to nurse the king's health."

"How fortunate for him that such a beautiful nurse could be found," came a saucy reply.

"We have heard that you are to keep him warm." The voice cackled crudely. Again, a chorus of cruel laughter hissed through the room.

"Tell us how you will keep him warm," one demanded. "Will you lie with him and warm him with your body and remind him of his pleasures with us?"

"One so young would not even know about such pleasures," countered a voice from far into the room. "Ask us what he likes. We can tell you how we satisfied his needs."

Abishag lay back on her soft cushions and silently begged for the queen's call to come quickly.

CHAPTER 6

THE DOOR CLOSED BEHIND THE queen. Abishag was alone with the king and not at all certain that he wished her to be there. She returned to his bedside quietly. Perhaps he had fallen asleep.

"You are still here, then?" His voice startled her.

"At the queen's command, my lord."

A slight smile crept across the king's lips. "That woman does have a commanding way about her, does she not?" A deep rattle in his chest tore the smile from his face.

"She is concerned for your comfort, my lord."

King David dug his elbows into the cushions and raised his head. "Indeed, she is! She refuses to let me die. I must wait for her permission." The faint smile returned, and Abishag knew his remark was a tender one.

"It is difficult to give up someone you love," Abishag said.

"Yes, it is," the king agreed. He settled back into the softness of the cushions. A deep sigh heaved his chest. "Well now, Abishag, why don't you tell me what you plan to do with me?" the king quizzed. His eyes were closed, and his breathing was labored when the coughing subsided.

Abishag busied herself arranging the great pile of blankets at the foot of the king's bed. The queen had also questioned her on her plan. For a moment, she considered the simple things she had to offer. If they did not suit him—or his Bathsheba—then perhaps Abishag would be dismissed and returned to her home.

"First, my lord," she began, "I will request that pots of water be kept at your fireplace day and night. Warm moisture in the air will take the chill from the room and also make your breathing easier. I will warm your blankets in the steam of the fireplace and keep them ready for you. In the mornings when the room is very warm, I will bathe you and massage your arms and your legs and your back. I will rub warming ointments over your body." She paused, but the king had no comment.

"I have herbs that can ease your discomfort as well," she continued. "And when it pleases my lord, I will play the harp."

King David opened his eyes. "My ministers should have found you years ago," he whispered wryly. "I shall look forward to hearing the harp again. Music does my heart good, child. But now my old body wishes to sleep." He moaned as he turned his back to Abishag and pulled the blankets closer.

Abishag looked about the great room and fit her strategy into the space. She directed the chamber servants to bring the pots of water. They heaped the fire with wood until their faces glistened with the heat. Later, the king's bed would be moved closer to the fire. She would have a cord strung above the fireplace where blankets would be draped to absorb the steam's warmth.

Heat from the blazing fire caused the silken robe to cling to Abishag's arms. Though she could not fault the luxury of the fine threads, she longed for her simple robes. With her rope belt, she could have pulled the robe up from her ankles and eased her warmth. She could have tossed aside her shawl, and her bare arms would have quickly cooled her. She reached down and removed the leather sandals. Her toes wiggled against the cool stone floor. Reasoning that she could not give comfort if she herself were miserably warm, she dared to remove her outer robe.

From behind the closed chamber doors, Abishag heard a noisy procession moving down the hall. A strangely familiar voice demanded the doors be opened for him.

"But my king is resting," the attendant warned.

"It matters not to me if the king is sleeping or carrying on with one of his women," came an arrogant reply. The irritation in his voice ricocheted through the quiet hallway.

The doormen bowed low as they pushed the doors aside. Abishag caught her breath when she recognized the man whom Joseph had called Adonijah. He strode into the king's chambers with the same impertinence that had spurred his horse through the crowded street.

Adonijah walked past Abishag without notice. "What is the purpose of this dreadful heat?" he shouted.

Facing his back, Abishag stood and bowed to the young man. "The heat is beneficial to the king's health, my lord."

Her voice startled Adonijah. He turned his angry face to find her. "Who is this?" he demanded of the doormen.

From his bed, the king delivered the answer. "Adonijah, my son, the young woman you have greeted so rudely is Abishag, of Shunem. Surely you have heard her name mentioned in the courts?"

The displeasure in the king's voice could not be ignored. It would not be in Adonijah's best interest to begin his confrontation with his father at such a disadvantage. "Forgive me, my father," he begged.

"It seems to me your apology should be directed to the young woman," the king replied. Abishag could see the muscles in Adonijah's neck bulge as he swallowed his anger.

"Of course, Father." He turned and bowed to Abishag. "Forgive me, my lady," he said with exaggerated obeisance.

"It is an honor to meet the king's son," Abishag said.

Abishag shivered as the man's eyes ravished her body. The outer robe she had removed would have at least covered her arms and hidden the soft curves that the satin belt so clearly defined.

Adonijah's desire sparkled in his eyes. "Perhaps we will meet again," he suggested. He returned to his father's bedside. "Are you feeling any better, my father?"

The king opened his eyes and looked at Adonijah. "I am well enough. What is it you need today?"

From the tone of his voice, Abishag surmised that this son visited only as his own needs arose.

"Father, Solomon has entered the king's chariot in the Jubilee races. He intends to compete in your place."

"He asked my permission weeks ago," the king replied. "The request could have come from you as well."

"But I did not think the king would allow such a thing!"

"You did not ask, either," his father reminded him. "Do you not have a chariot and horses fine enough to compete?"

"I do, Father. I shall make it a difficult race for Solomon. When I win, it will not be attributed to the advantage of the king's horses." Adonijah's fists clenched at his side.

"If you win, I shall be the first to applaud your horsemanship." The king sighed. "Make it a fair race, Adonijah, and all Jerusalem will applaud with me."

"I will win, Father," Adonijah assured as he turned to leave. His long legs confidently moved down the steps from the bed and past Abishag as if he had forgotten her presence. Abishag allowed a sigh of relief when the chamber doors closed behind him.

CHAPTER 7

Fully awakened, the king struggled to sit. Abishag moved to the bedside and repositioned the cushions behind him. He settled back into them and closed his eyes again.

"Adonijah lacks no self confidence, does he?" the king remarked.

"No doubt his skill merits it." Abishag feared revealing her contempt for the king's son.

"He is, indeed, a skilled horseman," his father agreed, "but Solomon is as well. It will be a close race. The winner will be the one who best motivates his horses to win. I dare say Adonijah's horses will be whipped with fierce abandon."

Abishag had gone to the fireplace and brought a steaming blanket. She pulled back the heavy cover and quickly spread the blanket over the king. The top cover was replaced over the warmed blanket and tucked close around the king's body.

"Ah, Abishag!" He smiled as the warmth enveloped him. For a moment, he seemed to sleep. Abishag studied the aged features of the king's face. His sun-weathered skin clung to sunken cheeks. When he smiled, sharp wrinkles fanned out from the corners of his eyes. His beard was thin and trimmed short, giving his lips a more active part in his expressions. Bushy white eyebrows marked the ridge of his forehead. His thick white hair lay matted from days in bed.

Suddenly, his eyes opened. Abishag marveled at the depth of the brown pools. If she ventured too close to this man, would she tumble into his soul and drown? A tired smile stretched across the king's face when their eyes met.

"Adonijah's mother has implored that I should proclaim her son to be Israel's next king," King David confided. "You have met him now. Do you wish him to be your next king?"

Abishag recalled Joseph's contempt for Adonijah. Perhaps Joseph's attitude had influenced hers, but it was difficult to ignore the arrogance that Adonijah radiated. He was full of his own importance.

"He is the king's son, my lord," Abishag answered at length. "Does custom allow us to question his rights?"

King David smiled at her simple diplomacy. "A king is allowed to do almost anything," he replied. "But he had best remember that every decision has its consequences, and those consequences are most often dealt at the hand of a bitter woman."

"Adonijah's mother is bitter?" Abishag asked.

"All my wives are bitter," the king admitted. "All except Bathsheba. She is my mighty oak. I never wonder if she stands on my side."

"Perhaps the king should have married only Bathsheba," Abishag ventured. Israel's royalty had been allowed the custom of multiple marriages—even marriages outside the Jewish population. The intent was to strengthen the nation by creating alliances with the marriages. The common people viewed the custom with disdain, however.

The king considered Abishag's remark. "Bathsheba was won at considerable cost to both of us," he admitted. "As much as I love her, I wonder sometimes if I would make the same choices, knowing all the grief to come."

"There would probably have been grief with any choice you made. Sometimes it is the grief that best acquaints us with our happiness." Abishag still grieved for her mother, but she was learning to replace the grief with happy memories.

The king sighed heavily. "Bathsheba and I have made peace with our God, but there are still consequences of my choice, all these years later. The rivalry between Adonijah and Solomon is but a single example."

"Solomon is your choice to be the next king?"

"He is God's choice, child," the king said. "And I have promised Bathsheba that her son would be the one to carry on the kingdom."

At the mention of her name, Bathsheba stepped through the chamber doors. The king's face brightened with affection at the sight of her.

"The servants talk of the heat from this room," she announced as she inspected the fire. "Does it please my lord?"

"Oh, yes," the king assured her. "Abishag has covered me with warmed blankets."

"What a clever idea to steam your blankets," Bathsheba admitted. "But the girl insures her position. Someone must replace the blankets as they cool." She smiled at Abishag. "You must have personal needs to care for. I will sit with the king for a while. You are free to go."

Abishag stood and relinquished the bedside to the queen. She pushed her feet back into the soft slippers and put on her outer robe, conscious of Bathsheba's watchful eyes.

"I will send for you later," the queen said as Abishag approached the chamber doors. "Perhaps you will be able to coax this old goat to drink his supper broth." She leaned to share a tender kiss with the king as the doors closed behind Abishag.

CHAPTER 8

Early evening shadows darkened the great hallway. Abishag tentatively retraced the path to the concubines' quarters. She paused outside the doors, wishing she knew the palace well enough to find a spot where she could hide from the vipers who had greeted her so crudely earlier. Instead, she pushed the doors open and entered the rooms that buzzed with mindless chatter. The quarters grew hushed again as her return was acknowledged. Abishag found her couch and curled up around one of the cushions.

"Look! The king has worn her out already," jeered the woman next to her. "Servicing the king is an exhausting pleasure, is it not?"

Wicked laughter echoed from all corners of the rooms.

"Tell us, Abishag," one concubine demanded, "are you so anxious to return tomorrow to entertain an old man?"

Abishag fought the urge to angrily reply to their venomous remarks. If she succumbed to their taunts today, it would become a sport for them. If she must live in their company while she served at the palace, she refused to be their toy. She maintained her silence.

"The king has sworn her to secrecy," one woman declared. "If she speaks to us of their pleasure, he knows we will expect him to call for us."

"That will never happen," came a loud reply. "After Absolom bedded us before all Israel, the king has refused to touch us. We are spoiled goods in his sight. Abishag is his virgin to heal his wounded pride."

"If only Absolom had overthrown King David, we would have been called for day and night."

"Absolom is a dead man," another voice reminded. "And we might as well be dead women. The king has locked up our wombs. Not a man in Israel will have us after we have been so disgraced by the king's son."

The chamber's air grew stifling with their bitterness. Abishag wanted to cover her ears with a pillow. She wanted to escape from their very presence. The king she had met today could not be the king these women had known. Abishag knew nothing of the pleasure for which they seemed to languish. Indeed, the pleasure they accused her of enjoying did not sound like anything she ever wished to know. She shut her mind to their words and slept until the queen returned for her.

CHAPTER 9

THE SOFT VOICE OF AN attendant woke Abishag. "The queen is here for you."

Bathsheba accompanied Abishag back to the king's chambers. "You have pleased the king," she reported. "I did not expect him to speak so highly of the nursemaid his ministers selected for him, but neither did he expect you to tend to his needs so carefully."

The queen's praise soothed Abishag's demeaned spirits. The one woman in the palace who might have reason to be jealous of Abishag's success was the only woman who seemed to understand the benefits the young woman might bring to the king. Indeed, Bathsheba seemed to welcome the comfort Abishag had already provided for the man she loved.

"The king told me that Adonijah paid a visit today," Bathsheba said. "I hope you will not judge all of his sons by that single encounter."

"Adonijah did not mistreat me," Abishag reassured. "His attention was quite focused on the king."

"No doubt," the queen agreed as the doors to the king's chambers were opened for them. "Here we are, Abishag. The king's broth has been delivered. It is important that he eat and drink. Do what you can to convince him." She turned and left Abishag to her task.

Abishag kicked off the slippers and removed her outer robe. She checked the fire and directed the attendants to add more water to the steaming pots. It was difficult to know if the king slept or only rested his eyes. She paused to listen to his breathing.

The king spoke as soon as she neared his bedside. "The queen has sent you to pour broth down my throat, has she not?" A faint smile played upon his lips.

"The queen worries that you do not eat and drink enough, my lord."

"The queen worries too much," the king muttered.

Abishag poured the steaming broth into the king's golden cup. "Would you enjoy going to the chariot races to watch your sons compete?"

The king looked at her in disbelief. "Are you suggesting that I might have the strength to leave this room and attend the Jubilee celebration only months from now? Impossible! Look at me. I can barely hold my head up to take your tasteless broth."

"It is not impossible, my king," Abishag countered. "If it is your wish, then we will begin to plan for it." She lifted the cup to the king's lips and tipped her head slightly to see if he would accept her challenge.

He did not answer, but he sipped the hot broth carefully. "Can they not bring me something that pleases my taste?" he asked.

"Tomorrow I will add some herbs to your broth," Abishag promised. "It will tempt your senses so that you beg for more." She smiled when the king looked at her doubtfully. "Wait and see." Then she changed the subject. "Tell me what happens at a Jubilee celebration."

King David's eyes sparkled with vivid memories. "It is a joyful festival of music and dancing, with endless feasts of foods seldom enjoyed in Israel. There are many competitions to heat the blood of the young men. And countless opportunities for the ladies to pass judgment on the beautiful gowns they all will be wearing."

Abishag offered the cup again, and he sipped without thinking. "What is your favorite part?" she quizzed.

The king settled back down onto the cushions. "The music and dancing delight young and old. It is in the soul to create music. But for some, the competitions are most enjoyed. There are foot races, and chariot races, and wrestling." He paused, remembering the years he had trained for the events. Abishag lifted the broth again. With this sip, it was finished.

The king glanced sideways at Abishag. "You are a clever girl," he admitted. He had been duped into draining the broth as they visited.

"No, my lord," Abishag objected. "I have never been to a Jubilee. It was fun to hear you describe it."

"Nevertheless, I finished the foul stuff. Be certain to tell the queen." He strained to adjust the cushions behind him, and Abishag stood to assist him. She held his elbow and pulled him to a sitting position. Then she fluffed the cushions one by one and repositioned them. She put her arm around his shoulders and gently lowered him back to the bed. She gathered a warm blanket from the fireplace and spread it over the king. With the heavy cover tucked close around him, he sighed contentedly.

"Would it please my king for me to play the harp?" Abishag offered.

He nodded in silence. All the conversation and the fuss with fluffing the pillows seemed to have exhausted him.

Abishag sat down on the step of his bed and lifted his harp to her lap. Her own simple harp was still packed away in her trunk. The sound from it would never seem quite as lovely again. The king's harp was tuned precisely to deliver music that touched the soul. She smoothed her fingers over its frame and across the strings. Then she leaned against the bed and began to pluck the strings.

Abishag did not know how long she played. She was certain the king had soon drifted off to sleep, but the soft music soothed her soul as well as the king's. She was not anxious to return to her quarters for the evening, but her duties here seemed finished for the day.

CHAPTER 10

ABISHAG HURRIED TOWARD THE CONCUBINES' quarters to escape the deserted hallway. Grotesque shadows danced in the light of the flickering torches. It had been a tiring day, and now she must return to her couch amidst all the sour women. Perhaps sleep would come quickly.

The quarters were quiet and darkened for the night. Someone not far from her couch breathed noisily. Abishag opened her trunk and felt for the cloth of her gown. Lifting the trunk lid released the smell of home, and the loneliness that she had avoided all day overcame her. She slipped the silky robe off her shoulders and dropped the woven gown over her head. The familiar cloth felt good to her touch.

How will tomorrow begin? she wondered. *Will the queen call for me early? Must I be attended in the bathing room again? Will there be more fine robes waiting for me? Do all these women have attendants to bathe them? Indeed, what do these women do all day if they have nothing to occupy them but their bitter thoughts?* Life in the palace hardly resembled the imaginations of the common people.

Abishag heard movement from across the room. Suddenly, her blankets were snatched away.

"Since you are so good at warming beds, tonight you can sleep without your blankets." Laughter echoed from all corners of the dark room. Exposed to the cool air, Abishag curled around her cushions and pulled them close. If only she were deaf like Jezreel! She would not have to hear the hateful things said to her. She closed her eyes and tightened her lips against any reply. She refused to play their game.

"You had better get your sleep. The king will be rested in the morning and in need of your services again."

"Imagine how busy you will be once his health has returned. Or maybe he will pretend to be ill forever, as long as he has you to comfort him."

"She can have the old man," a voice declared. "Who wants to be shut up in a room with someone who can no longer repay pleasure with pleasure?"

Utter bitterness permeated their words and their laughter. Nothing about the man she had met today seemed worthy of such hatred. These women could not possibly have known the king who talked so easily with her today and who smiled even through his discomfort. They apparently lived lives of ease in the palace. She had not seen any of them exerting a finger to contribute to their keep. Their chief complaint with the lot life had dealt them seemed to be that they had been forgotten by the king.

The room quieted. The taunts were finished for the day. For a few minutes, Abishag was free to think of home. Was it only this morning that she had told Joseph goodbye? How she missed Jezreel's quiet companionship and Nathan's ornery grin! She even missed her father's sad face.

"Are you awake?" a voice whispered close to her ear.

"Oh!" Abishag was startled back from her thoughts of home. "Yes, I'm awake."

"Can you go with me to the outer chamber?"

"I suppose so," Abishag answered cautiously. She had little reason to expect this to be a kind encounter.

The darkened figure reached for Abishag's arm. "Shhh! We must be quiet."

They picked their way through the couches to the door. The unknown figure pushed open the door and motioned Abishag to follow. A single torch lighted the room. Abishag saw that this woman was one of the older concubines. She had noticed her earlier only because she had remained silent when the others taunted her.

"My name is Rachel," the woman whispered. "I must apologize for the way you have been treated here today."

"Thank you, Rachel," Abishag answered. "There must be sadness for those women that I do not understand."

"Indeed!" Rachel agreed. "I will tell you sometime about the sadness. I only wanted to let you know tonight that I am sorry for the hateful things they said to you today."

"Would it be better for you if they do not know we have talked?" Abishag whispered.

"For now, it might be best," Rachel admitted. She slipped her arm around Abishag. "I hope it will be better for you soon. We will talk again."

CHAPTER 11

ABISHAG WOKE EARLY THE NEXT morning. Hoping to finish her bathing before the pool became crowded, she gathered up yesterday's gown and her hair combs. The steaming water would sooth her chilled body. The night had been too cool to sleep without blankets.

She pushed aside the curtains to the bathing room, as anxious for the seclusion of the room as for the warmth of the water. The attendants had arrived before Abishag and were busy preparing the room for the morning's baths.

"Greetings, my lady," they said in unison as they bowed.

Abishag's anticipation for a private bath quickly dissolved. "My name is Abishag. Please call me by my name. I shall not be allowed to bathe myself today?" she asked.

"It is the queen's command that we bathe anyone from these quarters who visits the king. She has told us that you will be with the king every day."

One of the attendants saw the silken robe in Abishag's arms. "We will bring fresh robes to you each day." She frowned at the simple bedclothes Abishag wore. "Sleeping gowns are available for you as well."

"There are times when old clothes are the most comfortable," Abishag muttered. She lifted the gown over her head and stood at the edge of the water. There seemed little point in objecting to their assistance.

Bathsheba fetched Abishag before the morning meal had been delivered to her quarters. Most of the women had not even awakened. Though hungry, Abishag welcomed the opportunity to leave before the jeering started.

"I am unable to assist the king with his breakfast this morning," Bathsheba explained. "It was reported to me that he finished his broth last night. Perhaps you can be as convincing this morning."

"I shall try," Abishag promised.

"Are your accommodations satisfactory?" the queen asked as they hurried down the great hallway.

Abishag could not resist turning to see if there was some evil smile lurking on the queen's face. Surely, she was unaware of Abishag's reception. "Things are done differently in the palace, your highness. I shall become accustomed." Frankness with the queen seemed inappropriate, but Abishag refused to pretend that the move had been inconsequential for her.

"It is the king's desire—and mine, of course—that you be comfortable while you are with us. If there is anything we have left undone, please let us know." Her words rang with sincerity. "Here we are," she said as they neared the king's chambers. "He is likely still sleeping, but there will be things you can do to prepare for the day. I will return later."

The doormen ushered Abishag into the king's rooms. When the doors closed behind her, Abishag sighed. Already this place had become her refuge. The most unlikely person in the palace had made her feel most at ease.

She hurried to the fireplace and found that the water in the pots had been replenished during the night. She gathered a few pieces of kindling and added it to the fire. The attendants could stoke it later, after the king awakened. Blankets had been hung to steam during the night. In the outer chamber, she found fresh towels and linens next to the basin.

"Bathsheba?" the king's waking voice asked hoarsely.

"No, my lord. It is I, Abishag."

"Oh, I thought you were Bathsheba." There was a hint of disappointment in his voice. "It is early for you to be here."

"If I am too noisy, I can come back later." How could the king know how eager she had been to escape to his chambers?

"You are here. I am awake. What are your plans for me today?"

Abishag dropped her gaze. She felt as if her presence was resented. "It is not for me to plan your day, my lord. I am here only to provide for your needs."

"What will keep you busy if I have no needs?" the king asked. He struggled to raise himself to look at her.

"If you have no needs, there is no reason for me to be here."

"Oh, you are mistaken," the king countered. "You are here because the queen wants you here. She hopes you will prevent me from dying."

"The queen wants you to be comfortable," Abishag argued. "Besides, it is impossible for me to prevent you—or anyone else—from dying."

"There comes a point when a person is ready to die," the king said.

"You are ready?" Abishag asked.

"My life has been a grand adventure. I have accomplished many things. Now, I am just tired. My body is tired. My mind is tired. Even my heart is tired. There have been a great many sorrows to endure along with all the adventure." His voice echoed with weariness.

"Then, if it pleases the king, it seems a good time for a massage. My mother used to claim my hands could chase away her aches and pains. Shall we see if my hands are so intimidating to your discomforts?" Abishag smiled gently when their eyes met.

"As you wish, child," the king allowed.

Abishag gathered a steamed blanket and brought it to the bed. She pulled back the covers from the king and loosened his bed shirt. She assisted him to a sitting position and pulled the shirt over his head.

"You mean to disrobe me?" the king teased.

"The best part of a massage is the oil I use on my hands, my lord. You will see."

While the king settled onto his stomach, Abishag poured oil on her hands and began to rub them together. The sweet smell instantly filled the room. Abishag closed her eyes and remembered massaging her mother's weakened body.

The king turned his head to face her as she worked. Abishag placed her hands on his neck and rubbed the tense muscles with her fingertips. Slowly, she worked down to his shoulders and began kneading the muscles with her full hand.

King David was not a large man, but he was well formed. He had been active in his later years and had never gained the weight of old age. Abishag's hands worked out onto his upper arms, massaging the arms that had once fought fierce battles and tenderly embraced lovers. It was not difficult to imagine this man with his lovers, but it was very difficult to imagine him pulling a bow tight enough to release an arrow to take another man's life. His passions seemed more suited to matters of the heart.

When Abishag's hands moved to the middle of his back, the king murmured a sigh of pleasure. "I think we shall do this every morning, child."

"We shall, indeed, if it comforts you," Abishag replied. She lifted the steamed blanket from his legs and applied more oil to her hands. "Are you too cool, my lord?"

"I have not been so warm in a long time," he answered. A slight smile played at the corners of his lips.

Abishag sat on the edge of the bed and lifted the king's foot to rest in the crook of her elbow. She wrapped both hands around the thickness of his lower leg and massaged deep and hard.

"How is it that a beautiful young woman like you is not married?" the king asked.

Abishag helped the king move to his back and pulled the covers up. She felt his eyes on her while she washed her hands in the basin and wiped them dry. He waited for her response.

"My mother became ill two years ago, and I was needed at home to care for her," Abishag shared. "I was to be married a year later, but my mother passed away only a few months ago."

"And now you have been sent to care for me?"

"It is an honor to care for you, my lord," Abishag assured him. "It is too soon, anyway, to ask my father to be happy for my marriage. He is very lonely now, and he finds little to laugh about."

"What about the young man you are to marry?" The king looked directly into Abishag's eyes. "Does he intend to wait for you?"

"Oh, yes!" Abishag's face brightened. "Only a few days before I left for the palace, he showed me the home he has acquired for us. His father is considered the best carpenter in Shunem. While I am gone, Joseph will build furniture for our home."

"You miss him very much, then?" the king suggested.

Abishag was uncertain how to answer this question. To be honest, she missed her sister and her brother and her lonely, unhappy father the most. "Joseph's family and mine have known each other for several years, but he and I have not had much time to become acquainted. It is my father's wish for me to marry Joseph, and I know he will provide for me. But I am content to wait until . . ."

"Until I die?"

"No. Until there is no further need for me at the palace," Abishag corrected.

The king smiled. "I am a stubborn old fox. I might decide to live awhile yet."

"That would make the queen very happy."

"Indeed!" the king consented with a sigh. "Have you brothers and sisters in Shunem?"

"Are you not weary from all this talk?" Abishag asked.

"If we are going to spend so much time together, I think I should know more about you," he answered. "You have the advantage. You must know everything about me that is worth knowing."

"In truth, my lord, there are countless things I would like to ask you." Abishag's boldness startled even herself.

The king pursed his lips as if considering whether or not her curiosity was sincere. "Very well, then. We will take turns. But since I have already asked a question, you will have to answer first."

"Will you agree to eat your breakfast while I tell you about Jezreel and Nathan?" she bargained.

"Do I have a choice?" he responded with a smile.

Abishag returned his smile and went to the outer chamber for the tray of food that had been delivered. Her empty stomach caught the smell of warm porridge, reminding her that she had been summoned from her quarters before breakfast had been served. She set the tray down beside the king and lifted the silver cover. There on the tray were two steaming bowls of porridge with hard rolls and honey and warm milk for both of them.

"So, the queen would not even allow you time for breakfast?" the king asked when he saw the extra food. "Then your stories of your family must wait until you have eaten. You will eat while the food is still warm."

"It seems odd to have my meals prepared for me," Abishag confessed.

"You are certainly not expected to do everything in the palace, child. You are, after all, a guest here. Now, sit down and enjoy your meal." The king's voice was commanding, even from his pillow.

Abishag knelt to sit on the step to the bed. Before she had settled into place, the king patted the bed beside him. "Sit here. I can't see you down there."

"Then we will eat together," Abishag said. "I don't like being watched."

"Nonsense," the king quarreled. "Every beautiful woman thrills at being watched. It gives purpose to the hours she spends plaiting her hair and choosing her robes!"

Abishag raised her eyes to the king. "I have not plaited my hair, and my robes were chosen for me."

"I see," the king said. "Well, it is a little-known fact that men prefer hair that flows freely. As for your robes . . . they have 'Bathsheba' embroidered all over them. She has excellent taste and has done well for you."

"The robes are much finer than my own, my lord. They seem too fine for me. I have thanked the queen for the many things she has provided for me."

The king seemed pleased with her praise for his queen. "Please enjoy everything she offers you. The robes are yours to keep. If there is anything else you need, you have only to ask."

Abishag broke open the king's roll and dripped honey over it. He reached out to take the bread from her and nibbled on it absently. Between bites, she offered him a spoon of porridge. At home in Shunem, her family would be well past breakfast. Her father would be at his market stall by now. Jezreel would be putting away the morning dishes. Nathan? He probably had already escaped to find his friends.

Breakfast warmed Abishag's belly. How thankful she was to be eating with the king and not in the concubines' quarters. She remembered her conversation with Rachel. Could she trust the kindness of the woman? Perhaps with time some of the other women would be kind to her as well.

"Is my bowl empty yet?" the king asked. "I do not think I can swallow another bite."

"Almost, my lord. You do not wish to disappoint the queen by leaving some of the porridge, do you? There is only a little more."

The king frowned but accepted the next bite. Abishag was certain he was not accustomed to relinquishing power, but his sigh was one of resignation. Had she already established such firmness in her duty that he knew it was pointless to resist, or was it important to him not to disappoint his queen?

"You have let your porridge grow cold," the king chastened. "Finish it now. I am ready to hear about . . ." He furrowed his brow. "Who was it that you were going to tell me about?"

"Jezreel and Nathan."

"And I want to know more about your father as well," the king prompted.

Abishag finished her meal and gathered the empty dishes onto the tray. "I thought we were going to take turns with our questions," she reminded him with a smile. "Do you get more turns than I because you are the king?"

"Of course, not!" he answered with a feigned irritation.

"Very well, then," Abishag continued. "My sister Jezreel is three years younger than I. People who knew my mother at that age tell me that Jezreel looks exactly like my mother did. She is beautiful! Her hair bounces in wild curls. Her eyes dance when she laughs.

She enjoys the simple things that most people do not even notice." Abishag paused for a moment. "And she is deaf."

The king's eyes flooded with compassion. "Was she born deaf?"

"No. She was very ill when she was four years old, and the high fever resulted in her deafness." Abishag swallowed slowly before she spoke again. "Tell me, my lord, do you think it was merciful of our God to allow her to experience the sounds of life for four years and then remove those pleasures from her?" Abishag could not disguise the bitterness in her voice.

"Child, sometimes our God arranges our lives so that we have no choice but to trust Him. I have come to understand that He uses everything that happens to draw us closer to Him. All unhappiness is not punishment. We mortals would never appreciate the beauty and wonder of life if God did not allow the contrast of sorrow."

"Sometimes it is difficult to trust Him," Abishag whispered.

"Often it is difficult to trust Him," the king suggested, "but He has only the best planned for each of us. Is Jezreel unhappy with her life?"

Abishag helped the king sit while she fluffed the pillow behind him. She put her arm behind his back and gently lowered him to the cushions. She brought a basin of warm water from the fire and soaked a cloth. Her warm hands pushed back the hair from the king's forehead while she bathed his face.

"Jezreel is not unhappy, but she has become timid. It is easier for her to remain in the security of our home than to force herself to go out into a world where she cannot communicate." Abishag paused for a moment, suddenly aware of the feel of the king's skin and the magnetism of his eyes. She looked away and dipped the cloth again in the warm water.

"Are there arrangements made for her to marry?" the king asked.

"My father is very protective of Jezreel. I'm not sure he could ever be comfortable turning her care over to a husband."

"But he must someday," the king said softly. "Your father will not always be there to watch out for her."

"She would be welcome to live with me," Abishag vowed.

"I think it would be difficult for you to trust anyone else to care for her. It is clear that you love her very much."

"I do, my lord. I will do anything I can to ensure her happiness." Abishag went to the fire to get a fresh blanket. "May I wash your hair, my lord?"

"How I wish I could stand beneath a shower of warm water and feel it run off my body." He looked at Abishag. "There are many things we take for granted, child. Many pleasures we do not recognize until we have to look at them from a distance we cannot span. Even simple pleasures like a shower of warm water."

Abishag smiled sympathetically. "Perhaps some of those pleasures can be experienced in new ways." She placed a sturdy cushion under the king's neck and removed the other pillows. Abishag reached around to support the king's shoulders as she set the basin of water beneath his head and dipped her cloth in it to soak his hair.

The king's hair was pure white with just enough wave for the water to curl the ends. Abishag dropped her cloth in the basin and combed through his hair with her fingers. With the tangles removed, she scooped up her cloth and rinsed his hair one last time. Abishag wrapped a towel around the king's head and rubbed the wetness from his hair. With the end of the towel she dabbed at the splatters on his forehead.

The king lay so still that Abishag thought he had fallen asleep. She found the king's comb and pulled it gently through the wet hair again and again. She had cared for young Nathan's hair, but there was something different about touching the hair of the king. As it dried, it became almost silky in her fingers. She bent to bury her nose in the freshness of the damp hair, forgetting for a moment that it was the king's hair that tempted her sensations so. Just as she moved to stand, she felt the king's hand on her shoulder. His touch sent an unfamiliar warmth through her body, leaving her cheeks flushed. The king's touch was so tender, neither demeaning nor presumptuous, just a tender touch that assured Abishag she had pleased him. It was beginning to feel very good to please him.

"Tell me about your Nathan now," the king reminded.

"You have not heard enough of my chatter?" Abishag asked. "Perhaps you should rest, and we can talk later."

"When I need to rest, there is nothing anyone can do to prevent it," he replied. "Until then, I am enjoying your 'chatter.'"

"Very well," Abishag sighed as she continued. "Nathan is six years old. I will always remember the look of complete happiness on my father's face when the midwife told him his third child was a son. It was not that he did not love his daughters. Mother always warned that Jezreel and I would become worthless princesses in our own eyes if Father did not stop doting on us. But it was Nathan, his son, who completed his life's dream."

The king smiled knowingly. "It is true. Sons are a father's most treasured heritage. But I have daughters, too, and I would not trade their soft laughter and gentle touch for anything in the world."

Abishag let her mind imagine the king with a small child in his arms. "You must have been a wonderful father."

"I have had much practice," the king replied, "but I have made some bad mistakes with my children. I sometimes forgot how to say 'no' when they demanded things that I knew were not for their benefit. Though mistakes can be forgiven, the consequences remain. I will tell you sometime about some of my mistakes. Perhaps you and your Joseph will not repeat them with your own children. Now then, I am waiting to meet young Nathan."

"Nathan has coal-black hair that curls close to his head. His hair is ornery, much like him. Combing it is futile. The curls bounce at whatever angle they like. But the curls frame a round, little-boy face, whose cheeks beg to be touched, they are so soft. And his eyes? Oh, my lord, you cannot imagine such eyes! They are pools of utter mischief that draw you helplessly into his childish fantasy world."

The king laughed at her picture of the boy. "You have described my Solomon as a child!" he exclaimed.

"I look forward to meeting your Solomon," Abishag said.

"He will be by. He comes every day," the king promised. "He is nothing like Adonijah. My sons shared the same father, but their mothers have influenced them as well—and their mothers are very different."

Abishag noticed the glow on the king's face when he spoke of his children. "When it is my turn, I will ask you to tell me how one man can care for so many wives and all their children."

"But it is not your turn yet," the king teased. "I think there is more about Nathan that I need to know."

"My questions can wait, then," Abishag conceded. "Nathan still thinks highly of his youth and regularly feels misused when his chores are assigned each morning. But he has learned that if he does them right the first time, he will have more time to play than when he is called back to finish a messy job."

Abishag sighed. "It makes me sad when I think of how much Nathan has missed out on knowing about our mother. He was so young when she became ill. A six-year-old boy still needs time on his mother's lap—time for her to convince him that he is a wonderful person, and time for her to teach him about life's sadness slowly. But maybe children accept death more easily than adults, who question God's fairness and try to understand every little thing about death. Or maybe a child just finds it easier to believe that they will be together again some day."

"It does take some time to make a disbeliever of a child," he agreed.

Abishag suddenly recognized the unhappy tone of her voice. She was here to comfort the king, not to *be* comforted by the king. "In a couple of years, Nathan will begin going to the market with Father each day. Until then, it is good for him to enjoy being a child."

"Nathan will become a fine young man, child. He might have lost his mother too young, but it is obvious that he has the protection and guidance of an older sister who loves him very much." The king reached out to touch Abishag's hand as she tucked the covers close around him.

For a moment, Abishag froze, uncertain how to accept or return the king's kindness. She raised her eyes to meet his gentle smile.

"Will you play for me now?" the king asked. "I will close my eyes and imagine that I am on a hillside with my sheep."

Abishag settled down on the step and gathered up the instrument onto her lap. She caressed the gilded frame. "The king's harp is too fine for such a one as me to strum its strings."

"I have never invited anyone else to handle my harp; but you played for me when Bathsheba first brought you to me, and your music touched my soul in places that have not known pleasure in a long time, even more so since you enjoyed playing the music." He paused. "Feel free to play the harp often. It will please us both."

Abishag leaned back against the side of the bed. She pulled the harp close to her and embraced its beauty. Could the king understand how the music flooded her with waves of rapture that lifted and plummeted her being so that it took her breath away?

"Do you not play anymore?" she asked softly.

"My fingers have become stiff and useless. Besides, there has been no one who cares to listen to an old man's music."

"What is so unpalatable about an old man's music?" Abishag asked. "It seems to me that an old man would have refined all the techniques for producing the sweetest sounds."

"An old man's fingers stumble over the strings, forgetting how quickly or how leisurely to pluck at them to best tickle his listener's ear."

"Perhaps one of these days we will see if your fingers have forgotten," Abishag suggested. "I dare say that when you feel the weight of the harp on your lap and touch your fingers to the taunt strings, you will remember what to do with them."

"Has Bathsheba instructed you on defying my age?" the king asked.

"No, my lord. You will find that I speak from my heart, not from the prompting of the queen, or anyone else." Abishag's fingers began to move across the strings, and the room bubbled with the gay music Jezreel always requested. Telling the king about her family had helped ease the loneliness she was feeling for them. Still, the worries she felt for them kept pulling her thoughts back to her home in Shunem.

A commotion at the chamber doors startled Abishag. It was Bathsheba's voice and a new voice she did not recognize. Abishag set the harp down and began to gather up the bathing supplies. The king had drifted off to sleep with the music.

The doors opened. Bathsheba hurried to the king's bed with a young man at her side. Abishag lowered her eyes and nodded to acknowledge them.

"He is sleeping, Mother," the young man noticed. "Must we wake him?"

"Old men would sleep all day if allowed," Bathsheba said with a smile. "He would be disappointed if you left without greeting him this morning. He has already asked twice if you had returned yet from the high pastures."

"I have indeed." the king agreed. A yawn stretched across his face. "How did you find the flocks, Solomon?"

So this was Solomon! Abishag stood back where she could watch without being noticed. While Adonijah's hair was a mass of free-flowing curls, Solomon's hair was cut short. Even at his young age, Solomon's face seemed leathered from days in the sun. His features claimed Bathsheba as his mother.

"Ramoth has cared well for your flocks, Father," Solomon reported. "The ewes are all bred and are beginning to grow fat. The high pastures are short, though, and Ramoth plans to move the sheep into the valley soon." Solomon smiled broadly while he shared news of his father's flocks. The king had been a shepherd first, after all. A shepherd's passion for the solitude of the pastures never dimmed.

"Water should be easier to find in the valley," the king said. "Tell me how your practice for the chariot races is coming along. Adonijah was here complaining that you have entered the race in my place."

"What Adonijah does best is complain," Bathsheba muttered.

Solomon smiled at his mother. "Adonijah will be a fierce competitor, Father. If his horses survive the practice. He whips them mercilessly."

"Someday he will learn that is not always the best way to get performance from his animals," King David answered. "Is your team ready?"

"Oh, yes! Jonathan has taken your assignment to care for the horses quite seriously. He insists they be fed at precisely the same hour every day. He has made certain they are acquainted with the weight of your chariot on their harness. We will be ready for the races, Father."

"Excellent. You have only a few months until the Jubilee." The king turned to Bathsheba. "Did I tell you that Abishag is going to send me to the celebration?" His voice sounded hopeful.

"Is she?" Bathsheba replied with raised eyebrows. "The people of Israel would certainly be pleased to see their king at the events."

Abishag had moved away from the king's bedside. He looked about the room until he spotted her by the fire. "Come, Abishag. I promised to introduce you to Solomon."

Abishag reluctantly returned to the king's bedside. She felt more comfortable knowing the king's family from a distance. Not even Bathsheba's fine robes could transfer to Abishag the air of royalty, nor the social skills she lacked to feel at ease in the palace. She always sensed Bathsheba measuring her abilities. But King David seemed never to mind her Shunamite phrases, and he made no note of the times she had failed to bow in his presence.

The king stretched out his hand to encourage Abishag to move closer. "Solomon, this is Abishag, of Shunem."

"Abishag, it is good to meet you. Mother has been telling me about you." He smiled warmly at her. "She tells me you play the harp, as well as care for my father's needs most attentively."

Abishag bowed. "It is an honor to meet you, my lord."

"I look forward to seeing Father's face at the Jubilee celebration. I hope he will cooperate with you." Solomon turned teasing eyes to the king.

"I have little choice," the king replied. "There is your mother to reckon with."

Solomon laughed. "What power a woman's will has over a mighty warrior!"

"You will see one day," the king predicted. "It is seldom the mighty warrior who is the real chief."

Bathsheba's eyes danced as they embraced the king's smiling face. "We should leave Abishag to her miracles," she suggested to Solomon. She leaned to share a kiss with the king and laid a soft hand against his cheek as their lips met. "It is good to hear your laughter, my lord."

Abishag had busied herself with the blankets by the fire. Intimacy was not for spectators. She listened for the big doors to close behind the visitors before she turned back to the king.

"It seems important to the queen and Solomon for me to attend the Celebration," he said. "We should not disappoint them."

What a difference this new motivation seemed to make! When Abishag had first suggested that the king attend the chariot races, he had snorted in disbelief. Her efforts would be considerably easier now that the king had someone to hold him accountable.

"You must eat well and sleep much," Abishag admonished. "As your strength returns, we must get you up a part of each day."

"How can I disobey such a lovely voice?" The king settled back into the cushions and closed his eyes.

CHAPTER 12

THE GREAT HALLWAY WAS DARK when Abishag made her way to her quarters for the night. Her steps were slow. She reviewed her conversation with Rachel. Even though Rachel had been kind to her, it was clear that she did not intend to openly befriend Abishag.

She did not hear footsteps behind her until they were very close. There seemed no reason to fear being alone in the hallway, and she had allowed her dread of the concubines' quarters to dull her awareness.

"Is that you, Abishag?" a voice demanded.

Abishag stopped and turned to see who was following her. Adonijah and a companion stood akimbo a short distance behind her. "It is, my lord."

"You stay late with the king," Adonijah observed. "Have you put all his other women out of his mind?" His voice reeked of ugliness.

"I stay until the king sleeps."

"No doubt you wore him out."

Adonijah's companion laughed crudely at the suggestion.

"Hopefully you have saved some energy for me," Adonijah jeered.

Abishag's heart raced as the two men advanced. She opened her mouth to scream, but the companion slapped his hand across her face in time to prevent her from making a noise. Adonijah grabbed one arm and his friend clutched the other. They backed Abishag against the wall of the hallway. Then he waved away the hand across her mouth.

"What a pretty face you have," he whispered so close to her face that she could feel his breath. With his free hand, he stroked her cheek. His hand moved over her body and fondled her roughly through her robe. Abishag closed her eyes tightly and swallowed her fear. A man's hands had never touched her like this, and she trembled to think what more he would do to her.

"Surely an old man like my father cannot satisfy one such as you," Adonijah said. "I will finish what he has left undone." He pressed his lips against Abishag's and forced her mouth open with his tongue. His hand reached around and pulled her close to him. At last, he relaxed his grip, and the men turned loose her arms.

"Tomorrow night you will come to my quarters," he ordered. "Elan here will be waiting for you outside the king's chambers." The companion nodded with an evil grin, no doubt hoping a chance with her would be the reward for his efforts. "Rest up this evening. I will work you hard tomorrow night."

Abishag backed away from the men and fled down the hallway. The roar of their cruel laughter chased her frightened steps all the way to her quarters.

Inside her quarters, Abishag collapsed against a wall. She gulped breaths of air between muffled sobs. Her heart thumped wildly against her chest. She pulled her robe close to her, remembering Adonijah's rough, groping hands. With the back of her hand, she swiped the taste of his breath off her lips.

She could not let the other women see her so disheveled. Who would believe that the king's son had mistreated her? There would only be more cruel jokes suggesting she had asked for the trouble she found. Abishag stood and straightened her robe. She dabbed at the tears on her cheek and pushed the stray hairs back into place.

When her feet felt steady, she slipped behind the curtain to the bathing room and filled a basin with water. She leaned down and splashed her face over and over. The cool water was refreshing on her flushed cheeks. She grabbed a towel and patted at the dampness.

A voice behind her startled her. "Is there something wrong, Abishag?" Rachel asked.

Abishag kept the towel over her face as she answered. "No. I am just tired, and I need to get some sleep." She folded the towel carefully and placed it where the attendants would find it the next morning. Rachel offered a tender smile and left to return to the common area.

In the darkness on her couch, Abishag's head spun with fears for the coming day. In spite of Bathsheba's overt distaste for Adonijah, Abishag did not feel comfortable reporting the incident to the queen. She certainly could not tell the king that his son had assaulted her. There was no one else who could provide protection for her the next night—and Adonijah knew it.

Her blankets had been returned to her couch, and she pulled them close around her. It seemed unusual that the other women had nothing to say to her, but it was a relief not to be at the center of their crude remarks. When she closed her eyes, Adonijah's sinister face danced before her. She could almost feel his grip on her arm. She pulled her knees up to her chest and wrapped her arms tightly around them, circling the private parts of her body he intended to claim. Finally, she slept.

CHAPTER 13

I NSIDE THE KING'S CHAMBERS, ABISHAG added kindling to the fire and made certain the pots of water had been refilled. She had not waited for Bathsheba to come for her this morning. If there were consequences for that, they would be paid. She felt safe with the king, and busying herself with the day's tasks distracted her from thoughts of Adonijah.

The chamber doors opened. "There you are, Abishag!" Bathsheba whispered. "Have you stayed the entire night?" There was an edge to her voice.

Abishag turned to face the queen. "No, your highness. I woke early, and it seemed pointless to waste time on my couch."

Bathsheba's gaze moved down Abishag's body, recognizing the robe she still wore today. "Was there no fresh clothing for you this morning?"

Abishag's gaze dropped to the floor. The queen did not sound pleased. "I tended to my own bathing this morning," Abishag replied. "This robe was not soiled." She remembered raw knuckles from scrubbing at home. Clothing was not washed until there was a good reason.

"Bathsheba?" The king had awakened.

"Yes, my lord," the queen answered.

"I thought so. Your perfume announces you." The king stretched out of his morning stiffness.

Bathsheba dismissed Abishag from her attention and moved to the king's side. "Good morning, my lord. Did you sleep well?" She leaned to share a kiss.

"I have slept better—after delightful romps with you." The king's frankness caught Abishag's ear. She noticed the queen's pleased smile at the king's remembrance.

Bathsheba sighed. "Romping is for the young. The aged must be content with memories. But what delicious memories we have!" For a moment, their entire world consisted of only the two of them relishing their oneness once again. Abishag felt like an intrusive observer

"Time now for your breakfast," Bathsheba announced. "Abishag is here to help you. Food seems to taste better from her spoon, so I will leave you in her care." She smiled at the king, patted his arm, and was gone.

Abishag carried the tray to his bedside. The king watched her remove the cover and prepare his plate. An uneasy quietness hung in the air between them.

"It is your turn to ask a question," he prompted.

A hesitant smile crept across Abishag's face. It would be difficult to keep from worrying about the coming night. How she wished she could tell the king about Adonijah's threats and call upon his protection. Instead, her mind raced to form a question to occupy the time.

"You will agree to eat while you answer?" Abishag forced a happy tone. "It seems that our king and our nation have an abundance of enemies. Do you likewise have many friends?"

The king pursed his lips as he considered his answer. "There are friends, and then there are *good* friends," he began. "If an old man like me can reflect on his past and name one or two good friends who have figured significantly in his life, then he is a fortunate man."

"Only one or two?" Abishag asked.

"Their rarity increases their value," the king replied. "If precious stones could be gathered by handfuls there would be no treasure in them. Nor pleasure."

Abishag offered another bite. "Do you consider yourself a fortunate man?"

"Oh, yes," he answered. "Many years ago—years before you were born—I met my first good friend. His name was Jonathan, and he was the son of King Saul."

"Did you play together as children?"

"Jonathan and I were young men before we met," the king said. "It was a difficult time in his life. His father had made some decisions that had harmed his favor with both his God and his nation, and he reacted to their displeasure with tyranny. Then, as any man would who must maintain his authority with undue power, King Saul began to suspect everyone of threatening his throne. He became bitter and moody and full of anger. That is how I came to meet Jonathan."

"I don't understand," Abishag confessed.

"The only thing that could soothe King Saul's unhappiness was music. Someone in the palace had heard of a shepherd boy who could play the harp, and so I was summoned to comfort the king. In the evenings when his body and mind were unoccupied, I played the harp for hours, until he was ready to sleep. During the days, I enjoyed the company of his son."

King David paused, then continued his tale. "Even as close as Jonathan was to his father, he could see how the king was becoming irrational. Since King Saul would not take counsel from anyone, especially not a son, Jonathan confided in me his fears for his father's sanity." For a moment, sadness washed across the king's face. Remembering Jonathan was clearly not an easy thing.

Abishag allowed the king some time and began gathering up the breakfast dishes. She added kindling to the fire and brought a fresh blanket to warm the king. From the steaming pots at the fireplace, she poured a basin of water for his bath. At his bedside, she pulled back his blankets and coaxed his nightshirt over his head. A slight moan of pleasure escaped as he snuggled close to the fresh blanket.

"Why did Jonathan not become the next king?" Abishag asked. King Saul had been Israel's first king, and there was no tradition to follow in naming his successor.

The king lifted wet eyes to meet her question. "Jonathan was killed in a battle. The same battle that took the life of his father." He swallowed a great gulp of sorrow before he continued. "The prophet Samuel had already anointed me as the next king of Israel long before that battle. It was God's plan, but King Saul hated me very much when he learned I had been anointed and would take the throne from his family. He devised countless plots to kill me. When Jonathan became aware of the plans, he warned me."

"It must have been difficult for Jonathan to remain loyal to his father when he knew he was scheming to kill his best friend," Abishag suggested. "How was he able to do it?"

"Truly loving someone allows you to overlook their imperfections," the king answered slowly. "And Jonathan truly loved his father."

Abishag wrung the water from her cloth and gently washed the king's face. Her free hand cradled his cheek. She pushed back his white hair and wiped his forehead. A fingertip smoothed his wet eyebrows back into place.

All the while, the king's eyes were fixed on Abishag. "Your touch is so gentle. I have watched a mother tenderly pat the back of a little baby to soothe him to sleep. Your touch is likewise comforting."

Abishag beamed at his praise. "I have soothed no babies, my lord." "When the time comes, your touch will easily hush a crying babe," the king said. "Until then, I will enjoy the benefit of your kind hands." His eyes twinkled now as he looked at her. He placed his broad hand over hers and pressed it tightly against his cheek. Abishag felt a blazing flush spread through her. After a moment, she awkwardly pulled her hand free to wring the cloth again. She had been caring for the king only a few weeks, but already he seemed to be allowing her into the privacy of his thoughts. He laughed with her. He asked questions of her to know her better. Now, he touched her.

Abishag had touched the king privately as a nursemaid would. Bathing the ill was a part of caring for them. Massaging aching muscles was no more than a way to relieve their pain. She had touched the king in those ways. But the sensation of his hand over hers was new and frightening.

Her mind stuttered over words to bridge the gaping silence. "Jonathan was a g-good friend to you," she stammered. "Has there been a second friend, one to take his place in your heart?"

The king's lips bent in a slight smile, acknowledging that he knew Abishag wished to move past the familiarity his touch had suggested. "Friends do not take one another's place in our hearts. No two people can exactly fit into the place of the other. My affection for Jonathan will never be assumed by anyone else. But yes, there is another good friend who lights up my soul in ways that even Jonathan never did."

"Does he come to visit you often?" Abishag asked.

"She visits daily," he answered, watching Abishag's face for recognition of his reference to a woman.

"It is the queen?" she guessed.

"It is Bathsheba, indeed!" His smile radiated affection for the woman he had named as his second good friend.

"You have many wives," Abishag remarked. *And many concubines,* she considered adding. "What makes your Bathsheba so different?" "Bathsheba is my last wife. She is a rare spirit. She understands me. She knows how and when to make me laugh. We can look at each other and know the thoughts between us. Bathsheba comprehends the power of silence and the good timing of disagreement. She is confident of my affection, so there is no occasion for jealousy with her. And, as you have observed, she forever wants the best for me."

"How did you become acquainted with the queen?" Abishag asked. She oiled her hands and began to knead the king's shoulders. She did not miss the heavy sigh before he answered.

"Child, the story of Bathsheba begins with lust and deceit, but through God's forgiveness, it has become a beautiful thing. The memories of my introduction to Bathsheba are painful for me, but it is good for me to be reminded occasionally."

"It happened one night when I was pacing the floor waiting to hear about the battle with the Philistines that day. Usually, I would accompany the army and be close at hand when the battle ended. But this was an uncommon period of dissatisfaction in my life, and I had chosen to remain at the palace during the battle."

He took a deep breath. "I had gone to the rooftop to get some fresh air, and I looked down around me at the homes next to the palace. Uriah was a captain in my army, and he lived close for security purposes. When I looked down at his home that night, I saw his wife bathing on her rooftop. It was a very warm night, and she was cooling off before retiring.

"I could see that she was very beautiful, and I had grown tired of the palace women. I ordered my doorman to summon the young woman to my chambers." He paused for a long moment. "A king can do that, but it should not be so.

"Bathsheba was very frightened when she stepped inside my door. I asked if her husband had come home from the battle, knowing well that he had not. I asked if she loved her husband, and she answered that it was her duty to love her husband. I interpreted her answer to be that her affection for her husband was merely obligatory, so I took her to my bed. She hurried back home in the darkness of the early morning, no doubt assuming that her body had been used for my pleasure once and there would be no further contact between us."

Abishag's hands halted momentarily while the king paused. Her heart fluttered at the story that was unfolding.

"There was, indeed, no further contact. I knew it had been wrong of me to summon her. A few weeks later, Bathsheba sent a messenger at night who told me she was with child," the king said. "My first thought was a selfish one—to come up with a way to conceal my part in her predicament. I devised the perfect plan to make the child appear to be the son of Bathsheba's husband.

"I sent a courier to my army commander with instructions to order Uriah back to Jerusalem. I would have him report to me on the battle and then send him home to be with his wife. But Uriah was an honorable captain. He refused to return home to enjoy the company of his wife when his men were at battle. He slept in the servants' quarters."

The king shifted while Abishag's hands kneaded his shoulders. "When I learned he had not gone home to Bathsheba, I planned a feast for the next evening. I would serve him wine and keep his cup filled until he was so drunk that he would not object to returning home. Again, he refused. My guilt then became desperate. My only resort was to have Uriah killed in battle. I dictated a message to my scribe and sent it with Uriah to his commander. My message was that Uriah be placed at the front of the battle, where he was certain to be killed."

The king shivered at this point in the story. "Uriah carried his own death sentence to his commander! It is painful to remember the

ugly desperation that prompted me to do such a wicked thing. But
the plan worked, and Bathsheba became a widow soon afterwards.
I was free to make her my wife, and I appeared honorable to take
Uriah's widow and raise his child as my own. Bathsheba and I both
knew this was not the case."

Abishag's hands halted again when the king became silent.
He seemed to be struggling with his next words. "Even though
God forgave me for the horrible sins I had committed, there were
those consequences I have told you about. Our baby died at birth.
Bathsheba was distraught. There was no way to comfort her. It was
punishment of its own kind for me to watch her mourn for the
child while she still mourned for her husband. There was grief for
me too. I did not eat for days. I was in foul spirits until I realized
that I would one day see the child again. Then it was more bearable."

Abishag covered the king's shoulders with a fresh blanket and
began to massage his legs. This man, the king, had made mistakes
like anybody else. He knew pain like anybody else. Though there
seemed to be many royal advantages in this palace, there were parts
of life that even royalty could not escape.

"Then Solomon came along soon?" Abishag begged for a happier
turn to the story.

"It took Bathsheba a long time to recover from the child's
death. For a while, she wanted nothing to do with me. I think
the immensity of what I had done finally struck her. I admit that
I avoided her as well. I could see the pain in her eyes too clearly.
Sometimes when we are hurting, we pull away from the people
who understand the best."

"The two of you obviously reconciled," Abishag said.

"Eventually, we began to spend time together," the king agreed.
"When she told me she was with child again, I wanted to shout for
her joy; but I was afraid there might be problems with the delivery
again. I was afraid to trust God's goodness. But Solomon pushed

his way into the world at just the right time and made his mother the happiest woman in all Israel." At last, a smile lit the king's face. "You have children with your other wives. What makes Solomon so special?"

The king shrugged, as if there were no quick answer to her question. At least, not an answer that could be explained with words. "One day you will find your own answer to that. From the beginning, Solomon was special in his own right. He has always had an uncanny understanding of what goes on around him. Beyond that, he was the first child of the wife I love. He brought her happiness, and in so doing, made me happy as well."

Abishag's hands stopped as she formed her next question. When the king broached a new subject, it was obvious that he did not wish to answer any more questions of the heart. It was confirmed when he broached a new subject. "If I am to attend the Jubilee in only a few months, shouldn't I be getting out of this bed soon?" He lifted his head from the pillow and turned to wink a twinkling eye toward her.

Abishag tucked away her questions for another time and returned his look with a forced smile. "You should, indeed! Not even a king can will his body to restored health after spending so many days in a bed, though. It will be a slow process getting you out of bed; but once your feet can carry your weight again—even a short distance—the progress will come faster. You'll see."

She gathered up the bath towels and organized her oils on the tray. Setting it aside, she pulled back the blankets so the king could turn to his back. Having done so, he lifted his hands to help pull the blankets close.

Abishag made no move to raise the blankets to his waiting hands. "Is there any reason why we cannot begin today to get you to your feet?"

The king lowered his arms in resignation. It was clear to Abishag that before she'd come to the palace, King David had been content to await death. No doubt there had even been days when he had wished for that solution to his discomfort. *Now, I'm asking him to challenge death and work toward strengthening the body he has given up for dead,* she thought.

Abishag had seen how delighted Bathsheba and Solomon had been with the suggestion that their king might attend the Jubilee celebration. Bathsheba and Solomon were the two people in the whole kingdom whom Abishag knew the king feared disappointing. It was probably of no consequence what anyone else thought of him.

He sighed, his eyes still closed. Abishag's heart skipped a beat. Was he now struggling with a new thought—that he did not wish to disappoint Abishag either?

"Tell me your plan," he said at last.

Abishag's face brightened with a joyful smile. "Today you will sit on the edge of your bed, but only for a short time. Tomorrow you will sit a while longer, and a while longer the next day. After that, when you are ready, we will touch your feet to the cool stone of the floor."

Abishag did not miss the king's soft sigh, one of acquiescence to her desires. "It will not happen if you do not truly want it to," she warned quietly.

"How can I not want it, knowing how much the queen and Solomon . . . and *you* . . . are counting on it?" A smile crept to his lips again.

"We cannot want it for you, my lord," Abishag responded. "Goodness knows, if the wish of the queen's heart could make you strong, you would be wielding your sword again this very instant."

"Then we must do something to lower her expectations." His smile now stretched across his face.

"The queen will be delighted to have you sitting beside her at the celebration," Abishag predicted.

"You will be there as well, will you not?"

"Knowing you feel well enough to attend will please me, yes," Abishag admitted. True, she had been assigned to help the king die comfortably; but in even the few weeks she had served him, she was beginning to understand the queen's reluctance to let him go. Abishag saw—or did she imagine—a look of satisfaction whisper across the king's face at her admission.

"Since you refuse to offer me my blankets," he said, "I assume that you intend to sit me up now."

"Now seems like a good time to begin," Abishag agreed. Their eyes met, and the king seemed to glimpse the challenges she promised. *Will he be able to accept mere mortal performance from himself?* Abishag wondered. *Will he be content with small successes? Can he forget for the moment that he is the king?*

In answer, the king lifted an open hand, requesting her assistance.

Abishag placed her small hand in his. *The Jubilee celebration will not happen without King David's attendance if I can help it!*

CHAPTER 14

By NIGHTFALL, ABISHAG WAS SO weary she wished to curl up on the king's rug and rest in the safety of his closeness. She had been promised a different sort of evening, however. Now that the king slept, it was time to find out if Adonijah's threats would be fulfilled.

She busied herself at the fire, straightening the steaming blankets and making sure the water pots were filled to the brim. She refolded the fresh blankets and tossed small pieces of kindling into the fire. The little noises she allowed did not stir the king. There were no further excuses for her to linger. She pulled her robes tightly around her and lifted the heavy handle of the chamber doors. A small gasp escaped her lips when she saw Bathsheba on the other side of the doors.

"Why, Abishag! I startled you. Forgive me."

Relief flooded across Abishag's face. "I was surprised to see you, that's all. We had decided you would not be visiting the king today."

"Has the king asked about me?" the queen asked.

"He looks forward to your visits, your highness. He knows only something very important would keep you away."

"Important, indeed," the queen agreed. "I must talk to the king, but then I will need to speak to you as well." There was something cold and disturbing in her voice.

"He is sleeping," Abishag whispered.

"Do you suggest I have no right to wake him?" Her irritation was clear.

"Oh, no, your highness. But it has been a difficult day for the king. He has been sitting up some today. I think he was surprised at how tiring it was." Abishag stuttered through her answer.

Bathsheba's racing urgency halted at Abishag's report. "The king has been up today?"

Abishag nodded at the queen's understanding. "Only for a few minutes each time, but he did sit. I think he wants very much to attend the Jubilee."

"Whoever would have believed that he might!" the queen wondered aloud. For a moment, delight hid the concern Abishag had seen earlier on her face.

"I think he wanted to surprise you in a few days and show off his progress," Abishag shared. She hoped the queen would humor his wish and not reveal that Abishag had bragged about his efforts.

"It will be our secret, then," the queen agreed. "You have done well, Abishag. He has not wanted much lately but to be left alone to die."

"He knows how much it would please you, your highness, and Solomon too. You provide his motivation."

"Solomon and I are not new to the king's chambers," the queen reminded Abishag. "It was you who suggested the possibility that he could attend the celebration. It was you who made him believe that he could."

"The king is not too old to enjoy a challenge," Abishag replied.

"Indeed," Bathsheba agreed. "Even old men rally at a challenge." She paused a moment, considering whether to wake the king. Her decision made, she turned back to Abishag. "Rachel asked to speak to me today. She told me about Adonijah's threats toward you."

Abishag's eyes opened wide in surprise. "How did Rachel know about Adonijah's threats?"

"She was returning to her quarters when she saw him back you up against the wall. She hid in the shadows and listened."

"She said nothing to me later," Abishag said, "and I did not tell anyone what had happened."

"Why were you silent?"

Abishag sighed heavily and turned away from the queen. "I was afraid everyone would assume I had asked for the trouble with Adonijah. The women in my quarters would have thought so, for certain. Besides, it seemed inappropriate to accuse the king's son."

"Adonijah has a reputation known to the entire kingdom, yet his own father cannot see him for what he is," Bathsheba spat. "How did you plan to avoid him tonight?"

"I did not know of any way to avoid him, your highness," Abishag confessed.

"Then you would have allowed him to force you?" Her eyes burned with a fury Abishag had never seen.

"I could think of no one to ask for protection," Abishag answered. The fears that had nagged at her consciousness all through the day now attacked her openly. Tears formed in her eyes.

"It is most fortunate that Rachel chose to speak on your behalf, then. I will not allow that disgusting man to touch you." Bathsheba glanced over to make certain the king was still sleeping. "And the king need never know. Do you understand?"

Abishag's tears bowed to the fierce anger in the queen's voice. "Certainly, your highness. Please forgive me for causing so much trouble."

"It is not you who has caused the trouble, Abishag." The queen's voice lowered and she pulled Abishag close to her. "You will stay in the king's chambers tonight. He is going to have a restless night, and he will need you to care for him."

Abishag looked again at the king sleeping quietly across the room.

"In fact," Bathsheba continued, "from now on, you will be staying in the king's chambers every night. Rachel told me how the other women have treated you. The king would be furious if he knew."

"What will the king think of my staying here?" Abishag asked.

Bathsheba sighed. "It will be necessary for me to tell him some of what Rachel reported. He is aware of the bitterness of those women. It is no secret that they despise him for neglecting them. He will want you protected from them. Of that, I am certain." She paused, noting Abishag's doubtful look. "It is not uncommon for a nursemaid to sleep close to her patient. The palace will accept your move without much question."

"As you wish, your highness." It was difficult for Abishag to hide her relief. Adonijah's threats were harmless now.

"I will talk to the king tomorrow," Bathsheba finished. "Do not leave these chambers without my permission. Rachel will bring you your things, and she will keep your bathing supplies and your clothing fresh."

The heavy doors closed quietly behind the queen. Abishag gathered some warm blankets from the fireplace and made a bed beside the king.

It was a restless night. Abishag woke early and sat up to stretch out the stiffness from sleeping on the floor. The silence of the room was comfortable. She need not hurry to the bathing room to avoid the remarks from the other women. She need not even be looked upon by their superiority. This room was her haven.

A soft knock on the outer chamber doors interrupted Abishag's thoughts. Before she stood, the doors opened. Rachel waited for Abishag to greet her.

"Rachel," Abishag whispered. "How good to see you. How can I ever thank you for speaking to the queen on my behalf?" She slipped into Rachel's outstretched arms and enjoyed the embrace she offered.

"You do not need to thank me," Rachel said. "I am happy that the queen agreed to see me in time to keep you safe from Adonijah. She does not normally make haste to respond to requests from our quarters."

"I suppose not," Abishag agreed.

"Adonijah is furious, no doubt." Rachel let her arms drop and stood back. "If he is intent on having you, he will not give up easily."

"I am safe here," Abishag replied.

"For now, anyway. But you cannot stay behind these doors forever." Rachel looked over at the king's bed. "Is he doing better?"

"Oh, yes," Abishag answered.

The pleasure in her voice raised an eyebrow before Rachel responded. "He is not dying, then?"

"It is not so imminent," Abishag assured her. "He wants very much to attend the Jubilee celebration."

Disbelief washed across Rachel's face. "Attend the Jubilee celebration? That is only a few months away."

"He will be there," Abishag vowed.

Rachel pointed out the soaps and towels she had brought, and hung the day's robe beside the bathing room. Her eyes slowly scanned the room. She seemed reluctant to leave. Rachel had spent time with the king in these chambers. A slight smile on her face suggested to Abishag that the memories were pleasant.

"It has been almost twenty years since I have been inside these doors." Her smile faded to sadness. "There was so much jealousy between all of us then; but when I was here with the king, he made me believe that I was the most beautiful woman alive! When he did not need me—those were unhappy days for me. I knew he was making someone else believe *she* was the most special of all."

Abishag listened silently to Rachel's remembering. The intricacies of loving a man were still new to her, but how different it would be if she were competing for Joseph's affection as Rachel had competed for the king's.

Rachel folded her arms around herself and turned her back to the king. "It does not matter now." She sighed. "My children have been well cared for, and my needs are met. I am thankful to him for that." A forced smile fell into place as she reached for the chamber doors. "Let me know what other things you need. Your trunk will be sent later this morning." She paused before adding, "You will be happier here, Abishag."

"Thank you again for helping me," Abishag replied.

Abishag checked to see if Rachel's visit had wakened the king. His breathing was still the steady, slow breaths of sleep. She would have time to freshen up for the day.

What a free thing to step into the bathing room alone! The king's arrangement was different from the bathing room in the concubines' quarters. There was no pool, just the choice of a marbled tub or the corner, where a warm shower could be provided if a servant raised the jugs of water. There was no servant now, and for that Abishag was thankful. Instead, she borrowed water from the fireplace and filled the tub herself. She slipped out of her robes and sank down into the soothing water. Finished, she stood and dried with the towel wrapped around her, just as she would have done at home. The opportunity for privacy was appreciated.

Steam from the bath water warmed the room nicely. Once dried, Abishag leisurely poured lotion into her palm and smoothed it over her arms and legs. She combed through her wet hair and pulled it back from her face. She gathered the fresh robes and dropped them over her head. She was growing accustomed to the feel of satin against her skin. Her supplies were neatly organized for the next morning, and the towels and wrinkled robes were folded and placed at the door, where she would later add the king's towels and bed shirt.

Abishag pulled back the curtain of the bathing room. Outside, she impulsively rose on a toe and spun around. This new freedom was refreshing. Her heart laughed within her.

"Abishag?" the king asked. "Whatever are you doing?"

Abishag's spontaneity instantly surrendered to the realization that she was being watched. She pushed her feet into the soft slippers and cloaked herself in her usual reserve. When she finally looked at the king, she found him sitting on the edge of his bed.

"My lord!" she exclaimed. "You sat up by yourself!"

"Indeed," the king agreed with a broad smile. "Did you fancy I should always need your arm to assist?" There was a happy tone to his voice.

Abishag hurried to his bedside. "Of course not, my lord. I was just surprised to see that you managed it so quickly."

"The room smells of a woman's bath oils this morning," the king said. "Why is that?"

Abishag stepped back. "I will let the queen answer that for you, my lord," she answered. Her move into his quarters must come at the queen's suggestion. Abishag had agreed to silence. She busied herself gathering warmed blankets for the king's bath.

"But the queen is not here." His eyes squinted slightly as he watched Abishag work.

"No, she is not," Abishag agreed. "She will come later. I spoke with her last night after you had fallen asleep."

"You seem determined to make me wait for my answer," the king said. "As you wish. While we wait, give me your arm and help me stand."

"You must have your slippers first. The floors are very cool this time of year." Abishag knelt and worked the leather slippers onto the king's feet. She had massaged his legs often enough to know that the muscles were growing soft. He would be surprised at the effort it would take just to stand.

Abishag was startled when she felt the king's hand on her hair. He lifted some of the damp strands and rubbed the hair between his thumb and finger, as if testing fine silk. "The curls in your hair beg to be touched," he said softly.

Abishag raised her eyes to the king's. He smiled warmly when their eyes connected. He let her wet hair fall through his fingers, and she tossed her head until the lengths caught behind her shoulder. A warmth surged through Abishag's heart and crimsoned her face. She looked away, uncertain how to disarm the sensation he had created in her.

Abishag stood and planted her feet securely to steady his weight. She gripped the king's arm at his elbow and held his wrist with her free hand. "Are you ready?"

"It is time to see what I am made of," the king answered.

He pushed himself up from the bed, but he allowed Abishag's gentle pull to ease him to his feet. For a moment, he lathered in the old headiness of success. Abishag watched his face carefully for grimaces of pain. There was only his broad smile and a deep sigh—a sigh she recognized as relief that he had not disappointed himself . . . or the companion at his side.

"Shall we go for a stroll?" he suggested with an ornery grin.

"Certainly." Their eyes met again, laughing together silently. The king lifted his hand to her shoulder, and they stood face to face.

Behind them, the chamber doors opened. Bathsheba halted abruptly in the doorway and gasped at the sight of the king standing at his bedside.

Abishag turned away from the king to greet the queen, but Bathsheba and the king's attention were entwined. For a moment, she feared the king might forget his limitations and shake loose to hurry and greet his beloved wife.

"What a sight you are, standing there!" the queen exclaimed. She pushed the doors shut behind her and swept across the room to the king's side. "How wonderful to see you up!"

"I was just coming to find you," the king bantered. Bathsheba slipped beneath his outstretched arm naturally. It seemed odd to Abishag—this triangled embrace. Though the king seemed comfortably fixed between the two women, Abishag's heart begged to pull away and retreat to a hidden corner.

"It would be best to be up only for a few minutes at first," she cautioned the king. "Let us help you back into bed. Then you and the queen can continue your visit."

"We will stroll next time, then," the king promised. He sighed heavily as he settled down on the bed. "You have come early this morning, Bathsheba."

Bathsheba glanced at Abishag with a look that dismissed her from the conversation she intended to have with the king. Abishag moved to the fireplace and busied herself replacing the blankets over the steaming pots of water, but there was nowhere within the king's chambers where she could not hear their conversation.

"I need to discuss Abishag's living arrangements," the queen began.

"Is she unhappy with the accommodations you provided?"

"Of all people, my king, you know how contrary the concubines can be when they choose. They have not made Abishag feel welcome. In fact, they have been unkind to her."

"What have they done?"

Abishag heard fury sizzle in the king's voice. Ever since Absolom had publicly forced himself on his father's concubines, the king had called for none of them. His son had attempted to overthrow the kingdom, and ridiculing his father by laying claim to the harem had been part of his plan.

"I will let Abishag tell you if she chooses. She has not spoken to me about it. Rachel begged an audience with me and asked on Abishag's behalf to have her moved from the concubines' quarters."

"Hmmmph!" the king muttered. "Rachel always was the only one of the whole lot who had a kind spot in her heart." He paused. "Where have you sent Abishag?"

Bathsheba bent her head. "She slept here in your chambers last night."

"Here?" the king asked incredulously. "There are no accommodations for her here."

"She seemed relieved to make do with what was available here for one night. If you do not object to our plan, we can provide a couch and other needs before the day is over." Bathsheba raised her eyes to the king's.

"You intend for her to live in my quarters?"

"My king, as long as she has been here, the girl arrives at your chambers before daylight to be here when you wake, and has not left at night until you are sleeping. Would it be impossible for her to just sleep here as well?"

Abishag did not miss Bathsheba's plea for the king's approval.

"It is not unreasonable to have her with you at all times," Bathsheba continued. "It is possible that you might need assistance during the night. With her here, I would not worry that you would be unaided."

The king turned to look at Abishag, who stood at a distance by the fire. "Will the court be unkind to her when it becomes known?"

"If what Rachel reported is true, nothing the court could whisper about Abishag could possibly hurt more than how the concubines are already treating her. People will think what they wish. You know that, my lord. If you and I and Abishag are agreeable to the arrangements, what other opinions really matter?" Bathsheba took the king's hand and stroked it.

"Very well," the king agreed at last.

When Bathsheba left, King David confronted Abishag. "Why did you not mention this to the queen?"

Abishag rinsed the washcloth and squeezed out the water before she answered. "It did not seem appropriate to complain about my accommodations."

"Why not?"

"Because I am your servant. I did not expect anything more than what had been prepared for me." Abishag bathed the king's chest and covered him quickly with a warmed blanket.

"*Servant?*" the king repeated. "You are no servant here. You are my guest. You have left your home and your family to take care of my needs. If you think you are a mere servant, then you have not enjoyed our visiting, and I presume you play the harp for me out of obligation rather than pleasure."

"You assume incorrectly, my lord." Abishag struggled to keep her voice even. She had not dared hope that the king had enjoyed the hours with her as much as she had enjoyed them. But neither had she dared imagine herself capable of providing him more than a reprieve from the physical ravages of age.

"Are you comfortable with the queen's suggestion?" he asked. He put his hand over hers to discontinue the bathing until she answered. "I am more comfortable here than anywhere else in the palace. If it pleases the queen and her king, then I am content to sleep here as well." Abishag pulled her hand free to resume the bath.

The queen had not mentioned Adonijah's threats against her to the king, nor would Abishag. Still, it was more the safety from the king's son than the relief from the concubines' company that made this change in living arrangements so fortunate.

"So, every morning now I shall be tortured with the clatter of a woman fussing and preening over herself in my bathing room?"

Abishag did not miss the laughter in the king's voice. If she had dared to meet his eyes, she would have seen the sparkle of mischief.

"And every night I shall be tortured with the interminable snoring of a man," she countered with a smile. "What an odd pair we will make."

Bathsheba returned in the afternoon with an entourage of servants bearing amenities that she quickly organized into a private area. The couch Abishag had occupied in the concubines' quarters was traded for a full bed of utter softness with layers of heavy blankets. The servants spread a sheepskin on the floor beside the bed. They assembled a curtained panel to grant her privacy. At the foot of the bed they positioned her trunk from home.

"What is all this?" Adonijah boomed as he entered the king's chambers.

Abishag froze at the sound of his voice. She had allowed herself to forget that he would still be visiting his father.

"We are making an area for Abishag to sleep," Bathsheba answered simply.

"Has Father's condition declined so rapidly that his nurse must sleep at his side?" His words were soaked in scorn.

"Quite the opposite," the queen responded. "The king is now getting out of bed with Abishag's assistance. If he should get up in the night and fall, she will be here to help him."

"That is reassuring," Adonijah quipped sarcastically.

Abishag felt his eyes groping her. She shuddered at the memory of his hands pressing her against the wall. He acknowledged her discomfort with a sneer that promised he still intended to fulfill his plan.

"The palace buzzes with the anticipation of seeing you at the Jubilee celebration," Adonijah reported to his father.

"How could I miss the competition between my sons?" The king smiled broadly as Adonijah approached his bed.

"Whose chariot will you cheer?" Adonijah asked cleverly. "It would not do for the king's chariot to be defeated."

"I will applaud the winner—whichever one of you it might be. One of the king's sons will be the champion, and my honor will remain intact."

"You are such a diplomat, Father," Adonijah observed with a laugh. He lowered his voice and nodded toward Abishag. "It will not be too painful to have such a beautiful woman sleeping in your quarters?" Again he laughed crudely.

"A man never gets too old to enjoy looking, Son," the king agreed. "At my age, looking is all I can do. I defer to you young men the pleasures of participation."

Adonijah nodded. Abishag watched him slyly purse his lips at this permission granted by the king to enjoy a woman. She knew it was not just any woman Adonijah intended to enjoy. It would be Abishag.

CHAPTER 15

Nathan woke early to the sound of his father's coughing. It was worse this morning, coming from deep within his chest. And it did not stop. Nathan pushed back the warm blankets and hurried to Jezreel's bed. Before Abishag left, he sometimes took his waking fears to her bedside and slipped in beside her to snuggle them away. Since she had been gone, he had resolutely shouldered his own six-year-old concerns. He had found that Jezreel's embrace lacked the comfort of his older sister's, but this morning he needed someone to reassure him that his father was not dying.

Nathan softly tapped his sister's shoulder. Jezreel stirred lazily, but sat upright when she realized Nathan had wakened her. His face was covered with fear. He motioned for her to follow him. Jezreel pulled on her woolen slippers and stood to see where he would lead her.

Nathan stopped at the door where their father slept. His dark eyes locked with Jezreel's as he put his hands to his neck and feigned a violent cough. He pointed to their father, hoping Jezreel understood his motions. She nodded. Their father's condition had grown serious.

Eliezer had not gone to his market stall for a week now. For the last two days, he had not even left his bed. The broth that Jezreel warmed for him was left untouched. And, though she could not hear the coughs that wracked his body, the utter pain that possessed his face told Jezreel that his illness was worsening. This morning she would send Nathan to find Joseph. He would know what to do. *How I wish Abishag was home!*

Jezreel moved quietly to her father's bed. She placed a palm against his forehead just as Abishag would have done. His face was hot, and moist with perspiration. He did not open his eyes. Jezreel tucked his blankets close around him and turned back to Nathan. How could she make Nathan understand that he must hurry and find Joseph? Perhaps it would be easier for her to go. It was still early enough that Joseph would not have left with his father for the carpentry shop.

At the doorway, Jezreel pointed her fingertips to her chest and quickly moved them down her body, the sign to Nathan that she was going to get dressed. Nathan waited impatiently by the fireplace. At the door, Jezreel grabbed her woolen shawl and wrapped it tightly around her. She pointed to the wooden rocker that Joseph had given them when their mother was so ill. Nathan would understand that she was going to get Joseph.

The morning air was frigid. The sun had not yet peeked over the horizon, but there was light enough to see where she walked. Her steps were quick and fearful as she headed for Joseph's house across the village. By the time she reached his door, Jezreel was panting for breath. She knocked urgently, knowing the family would still be sleeping.

Joseph's father came to the door. His sleepy face was flushed with anxiety at the early morning knock. "Jezreel! Why are you here?" His question became words, even though Jezreel could not hear him. He quickly motioned her to come into the house. Jezreel shook her head and pointed inside the house and then waved her arm to beg someone to follow her home.

"Do you need Joseph to come?" he guessed aloud. He held a finger up to ask Jezreel to wait while he woke his son. She stepped inside the door and waited nervously, aching to get back to her father's side.

Joseph hurried from the back room, still tying the sash around his robe. Only an emergency would bring Jezreel to his door, and there would be no way to know the cause until he arrived wherever she took him. He grabbed a cloak and threw it around his shoulders as they started out the door.

Joseph found himself fairly running to keep up with Jezreel. The morning wind whipped at her robes and tangled them in her legs, but her pace did not falter. It soon became evident that she was leading him to her father's house. When they neared the house, Nathan pushed through the door and ran to meet them.

"What has happened?" Joseph asked the young boy.

"Father is very ill. I think he might even be dead." Nathan choked over the words. Joseph's eyes met Jezreel's, and all the fear he had seen there before became clear to him. Jezreel pulled Nathan close and patted him tenderly on the back.

Could Eliezer be dead? Joseph was glad Jezreel had not heard the boy's words.

Spurred on by a better understanding of the emergency, Joseph rushed into the house. Jezreel was close behind and ran ahead to lead him to her father's bedside. Joseph approached the quiet form with dread. What if Nathan was correct? What if Eliezer was dead?

Jezreel sat down on the edge of the old man's bed. Oblivious to Joseph's fear, she reached out a soft hand to stroke her father's cheek. Joseph's breaths were suspended, waiting for some sign of life. As if on cue, Eliezer's eyes fluttered at the touch of his daughter, but there was no strength to keep them open. As suddenly as he stirred, he returned to his sleep.

Joseph touched young Nathan's shoulder and led him out of the room. "Run and ask my mother to come," he commissioned the boy. Nathan seemed relieved to have an assignment, something he could do to help care for his father. Joseph watched the little legs sprint away. Nathan would, no doubt, run the whole distance.

When the child was out of sight, Joseph tended the fireplace. His thoughts turned to Abishag. She would want to know about her father. Indeed, she would probably insist on coming to care for him. Jezreel would want that. For her sake, he would find a way to get word to Abishag.

Joseph stood at the doorway watching Jezreel. She had assumed Abishag's household responsibilities out of necessity, although timidly at first. Now, after several months, Jezreel seemed to move through her tasks more confidently. There were even occasional smiles for him when he stopped by, but her thoughts were sealed tightly in her heart. Would anyone ever be able to loosen her grip on her feelings?

For a while after Abishag left, Joseph had stopped by Eliezer's house daily. His promise to watch out for Jezreel was fresh in his mind. Later on, however, his visits became less frequent. It was awkward to be the guardian over a deaf girl who kept herself closed up from him like a beautiful rose bud, whose petals clung protectively around the heart of the flower.

At last, Nathan returned with Joseph's mother firmly attached to his little hand. Joseph quickly related his assessment of Eliezer's condition to his mother. Miriam frowned. The symptoms were familiar. It had been a difficult winter. Already many had died from this cough.

Miriam tapped Jezreel's shoulder and took her place at Eliezer's bedside. She touched his forehead. His skin was pale, and his cheeks were sunken from lack of fluids. His breaths were shallow and interrupted with long minutes of coughing.

"I think you should send for Abishag," Miriam said. "Joseph, if you leave now you can be back by this evening."

Joseph went to Jezreel and held her by the shoulders. He looked into her eyes as he had seen Abishag do so often. He said simply, "Abishag," and motioned that he was leaving. Jezreel nodded her understanding. Her cheeks were damp with tears.

Joseph spurred his donkey through the crowded streets of Jerusalem. He was exhausted from the trip, but the memory of Jezreel's sad face urged him on. Miriam was expecting the worst or she would not have sent Joseph to bring Abishag home. Even Jezreel had understood that much.

At the palace gates, Joseph announced that he must see Abishag, the Shunamite who was caring for the king. The guards ushered him to a waiting area and sent for Abishag. Several minutes passed before he heard her voice.

"Joseph!" Abishag cried. "What has happened? Why are you here?"

For a moment, Joseph stared at the woman who had been summoned to him. This woman was dressed in silken robes, and her hair flowed freely over her shoulders. Abishag had been beautiful to him in her rough woolen robes. Here she stood now dressed in silk. He felt too common to touch her. His arms hung limply at his sides.

"Your father is very ill," he finally answered. "Mother sent me to bring you home. It is the bad cough. Many in our village have died this winter."

"How long has he been ill?" she questioned impatiently.

"Nathan said he has been sick a long time; but to a six-year-old, a couple days can be a long time." Joseph knew his vague answer was no help to Abishag, and he did not want to admit that he had not been by Eliezer's house in almost two weeks. Would she be angry with him for not coming sooner?

"I will pack a bag and be ready to go shortly," Abishag decided. "Wait for me here."

"Abishag," Joseph said softly, "you will need to change your clothing. You cannot travel on a donkey in such fine robes."

Abishag looked down at her robes. "I will change, of course. We must travel with haste."

Abishag hurried through the hallways to the king's chambers. It was the worst time for her to leave the king. He was gaining strength, and he needed to continue being up a part of each day. As faithful as Bathsheba was to visit, she seemed to have too many court responsibilities to be free to spend long periods of time with the king. But Abishag had no choice.

"My lord, I have been called home to tend to my father. He has been ill for several days. Joseph has come for me," she explained rapidly. Without waiting for his response, she began pulling clothing from her trunk. Behind the curtained panel, she shivered out of the silk robes and slipped her woolen robe over her head.

"I will send you in a carriage," the king declared. "It will be more comfortable for you to travel that way. You must send word about your father back to me with the horseman."

"Joseph brought a donkey for me," Abishag said.

"He is welcome to ride in the carriage with you. I can have the donkeys delivered back to him later." Seeing hesitation on Abishag's face, the king continued, "Please let me do this for you."

"I do not know how Joseph will feel about it," Abishag said.

"He loves you, and he will want you to get home to your father as quickly and as comfortably as possible. He has just traveled hard to get to you. I predict he will be grateful for the offer." The king smiled at Abishag's indecision. "Get the doorman, and I will send him to order the carriage."

The doorman was called, and the king dispatched him immediately. Abishag gathered up the things she had chosen to take. She was anxious to get to her father, but it would be difficult to close the door behind her here.

"Come here, Abishag," the king called. She stood awkwardly beside his bed. The king took her hand and raised her palm to his lips. He kissed the soft skin. "I pray for a safe trip for you and Joseph. I pray that your father recovers and lives to see you happily married. When you are comfortable with his condition, I look forward to welcoming you back to the palace."

"Thank you, my lord. It is not easy to leave you." Abishag battled the tears that spilled out of her heart.

"You will return. There is that to anticipate," the king suggested.

"When I come back, we will go for a stroll." Abishag forced a smile to her voice. "Until then, please take care of yourself."

"Joseph is waiting," he replied.

Joseph did accept the king's offer of a carriage. Abishag watched as he settled down into the seat opposite her. Such cushioned luxury was foreign to him, but he soon found a comfortable position and turned his attention back to her.

"Jezreel will be relieved to have you home," he said.

"Has she done well without me?" Abishag's arms ached to wrap around her sister.

"She seems more comfortable with her tasks now," Joseph answered. "It is your companionship that she misses. I'm not sure she is willing to let anyone take your place."

"It takes a long time to learn another's language, I suppose." Abishag rushed to excuse Jezreel's aloofness. She and Jezreel had been close ever since the young girl's world had gone silent. "And Nathan—is he happy?"

"Nathan is fine," Joseph reported with a smile. "We have gone fishing, and he sometimes comes to Father's shop to watch us work. Father gave him a chisel and a hunk of worthless wood for him to sculpt. I think his hands are better suited to carpentry than tending a fish stall."

"Father will be disappointed if Nathan does not join him at the fish stall," Abishag countered.

Joseph sighed and laid his head back against the softness of the cushions. "Your father seemed pleased for us to spend time together. He wants the boy to be happy."

It was true. Eliezer's happiness seemed to have shriveled away since his wife died. He wrapped his sorrow around himself and tromped miserably through each day. He would be relieved to abandon the bothersome antics of the child over to someone who had the energy to enjoy him.

Joseph's breaths soon slowed to sleep's pace. Abishag stared at this man who was to be her husband. In truth, she had grown comfortable enough in the palace that she had little need to salve her loneliness with thoughts of him. Joseph was a good man, and he would tend to her needs carefully. However, the king was far from dead, and her commission at the king's bedside continued to his death.

Earlier, Joseph had inquired about the king's health. Abishag had not missed the droop of his shoulders when he understood that her permanent return home would not be soon. In fact, there had been an awkward silence between them then. Abishag wondered if he might not be considering breaking their betrothal. He would have legal reason for doing so. Perhaps she should bring the matter up and provide him his opportunity for freedom.

The carriage moved along quickly. Darkness was settling upon them when Abishag saw the familiar outskirts of Shunem. Even stretched out across the horizon, the city seemed small, but there was a sense of coming home when they entered the city limits. She scooted to the edge of her seat and peered out the window with renewed enthusiasm.

"Joseph, we are in Shunem," Abishag whispered. She reached out gently to wake him.

"Already?" he asked incredulously. "I must have slept for hours. Forgive me for being such rude company."

"You were weary from your fast ride to Jerusalem. You made the trip on my behalf." Abishag paused as she considered the effort he had made. "I am pleased you were able to rest on the trip home. There will be time for us to visit later."

The carriage slowed and stopped just inside the city. Joseph climbed down and straightened his robe before he approached the driver. "If I may sit with you, I will give you directions to the young woman's home."

Alone in the carriage, Abishag acknowledged her own weariness and leaned her head back against the cushion. Joseph had carefully described Father's condition. It would be difficult to see him so ill. She could easily imagine how frightened Nathan must be. And Jezreel too.

It was not long before the carriage pulled up to Eliezer's home. Joseph hurried down to the ground and opened the door for Abishag. She took the hand he offered and stepped out of the carriage. For a moment, she stared at the house before her. Such a strange mixture of dread and anticipation battled inside her! Fall had turned into winter since she had left for the palace. It would be so good to see her family again.

"Nathan will be watching for you," Joseph predicted.

As if on cue, the front door opened, and the little boy raced to greet his sister. His arms wrapped around her waist, and he snuggled close as she returned his embrace.

"Oh, Abishag!" he cried, "I have missed you so much!"

Abishag pulled free of his arms and knelt down to look into his face. "It is so good to see you again, little brother!" He buried his face in her neck and locked his hands around her neck.

"Joseph tells me you have been a big help to Jezreel. I am proud to hear that," Abishag exclaimed.

"Jezreel missed you too," Nathan replied. "But we have managed. Father says we make a good team."

"Let's get inside out of this cold weather and see how Father is doing," Abishag suggested. She stood and took Nathan's small hand in hers. He pulled her toward the house anxiously. Joseph followed in silence. *How severe is the situation that awaits me?* Abishag asked herself with a shudder.

Just inside the door, Joseph's mother hushed them. "Eliezer is sleeping," she explained, "and Jezreel has drifted off to sleep as well. She has refused to leave your father's side all these hours."

Abishag hurried past Miriam and went to her father's room. She paused in the doorway and found Jezreel curled up on the floor, her head resting on Father's bed. Touching Jezreel would startle her, but perhaps the touch of her sister's hand would provide welcomed relief. Abishag knelt on the floor beside Jezreel and took her sister's hand.

Jezreel woke instantly. Her eyes widened at the sight of Abishag. Abishag wrapped her arms around her sister's shoulders and pulled her close. How good it felt to embrace her! Abishag might have ignored the pain of separation from Jezreel while she was busy at the palace, but now her heart groaned over the weeks they had been apart. Her hands grasped Jezreel's shoulders and pushed her back so their eyes could meet. She saw the fear that Jezreel could not speak. She pulled her close, and their hearts comforted each other. Abishag looked over Jezreel's shoulders to her father on the bed. His breaths were wheezes, and the pallor of death possessed his face. It was clear that he would not recover from this illness. His children would lose another parent so soon, and life would become complicated in new ways.

Jezreel moved away to allow Abishag closer to their father. Abishag wrapped her hand around Eliezer's limp hand and pressed it to her cheek. Tears spilled over onto her father's robe. Her grip around his fingers tightened as if to deny his passing. Joseph quietly offered Jezreel his hand, and he cleared the darkened room of all but Abishag and her father.

Abishag crumbled to the floor at his bedside. Her shoulders heaved as her sorrow spilled from her heart. "Oh, Father," she sobbed, "I love you so dearly. How can we let you go?"

Startled by a weak squeeze from her father's fingers, Abishag pulled her head up to find her father's eyes on her. Tears slipped down the creases in his aged face as he watched his eldest child seek comfort at his side.

"I love you, too, Daughter," he whispered.

"Let me help you recover from this," Abishag begged.

"It is my time," came his reply. "Care for Jezreel and Nathan."

Abishag wiped her face with a corner of her shawl. Her father was entrusting the responsibility of the family to her. This one last thing she could do for him. "You know I will provide for them."

Her father coughed violently, and Abishag feared there would be no strength for him to say more. He swallowed a great gulp of air before he continued. "The palace commission—it is yours."

"I don't care about that, Father."

"Use it for the family," her father instructed weakly, each word a struggle. "It is hidden in your mother's trunk. I wish I . . ." Eliezer's fingers suddenly fell limp in Abishag's hand. She did not raise her eyes to his face, but she knew he was gone.

CHAPTER 16

In THE NIGHT HOURS WHEN Abishag wrestled silently with her thoughts, the only logical solution she could find to her family's situation was also a painful one for her. Eliezer had been buried a week earlier, and now there was the matter of finding someone to care for Jezreel and Nathan. If Abishag asked the king, she was certain he would release her from her responsibilities at the palace to allow her to return to Shunem. But in those quiet moments of aloneness, she admitted that she did not want to leave the palace and the friendship she had found with the king.

And so it was that Abishag devised a time to speak to Joseph. The constant flow of family and friends to the house of Eliezer had slowed soon after the funeral. Finally, there came opportunities for the two of them to visit privately. It was a hard thing she would ask of Joseph.

"I cannot tell you how much longer I will be at the palace," she began. Joseph lowered his head and bit back any hasty words. Abishag did not miss the tightening of his jaw. She had made it clear that she would not default on her commission to the king. It seemed Joseph would forever be waiting for someone to die before their marriage could take place. "It has already been too long to ask you to wait for me."

Abishag paused awkwardly, wishing that what she must say could be understood without words. It could not. There must be no chance that Joseph would misunderstand what she was asking. "Nathan has become very attached to you," she continued. "His face brightens when he sees you, and he chatters at great length about the things the two of you have done together."

"I have not wanted him to miss out on his childhood," Joseph explained. "He has already had to shoulder many sorrows that would stagger an adult."

"And Jezreel? I can see that she is more comfortable in your presence."

"She seems to be," Joseph agreed.

"It appears that she has handled the household responsibilities here quite remarkably." Abishag looked intently at Joseph. Was he beginning to recognize the path her thoughts were traveling?

"She has done very well," he said.

"If it were not for her deafness, she would have been married by now." Abishag paused again, this time waiting for boldness to continue. "She is beautiful, don't you think?"

Joseph jerked his head up to meet her eyes. He understood. Abishag felt a strange mixture of relief and disappointment that he did not immediately protest her suggestion.

"She has an inner beauty that few see," he said.

Abishag turned away. "Indeed. And because you have seen her beauty, it is easier for me to ask you to consider marrying her." Her heart pounded wildly. She had always claimed she would give anything to protect Jezreel's happiness. She had just sacrificed her own marriage.

"But you and I are betrothed," Joseph whispered incredulously.

"We are," Abishag agreed. "But there is a better opportunity for you with Jezreel, if you will accept it."

"If you and I would marry, Jezreel and Nathan could live with us." Joseph reached for Abishag's arm and pulled her to face him. Tears bulged at the corners of her eyes.

"But you and I cannot be married. Not right now. And right now, Jezreel and Nathan need a home."

"And it would please you if I married Jezreel and raised Nathan as if he were my son?"

"Would that be so difficult for you?" Abishag's words held a brittle edge. She had rehearsed this scene often enough in the night, and she wished for it to be over.

"Would that be so easy for you?" Joseph countered. "Before we decide the fate of your sister and brother, you had better be sure that you are not jeopardizing your fate as well as theirs."

Abishag squared her shoulders and considered her words carefully. "I would never worry about Jezreel and Nathan if they were in your care. For now, that is the most important thing to me."

"But eventually King David will die, and *you* will need a home. How will you feel about this bargain then?" Joseph's eyes drilled through her resolve to hide her heart from him.

"Joseph, I cannot see into the future. The king might well live another year, or two, or even five. Whenever my services are no longer needed at the palace, then I will have to deal with the problem of being unmarried." Abishag could not face him. "Until then, I am committed to the king. I would be most grateful if you would take Jezreel as your wife and help raise Nathan as your son."

Joseph held his answer for a moment. He paced around the room, pausing at the door to Nathan's room. Indeed, it had been amusing to have the innocent curiosity of a child to keep him company at his father's shop. Oh, the questions he could ask! Remembering Nathan's wide-eyed excitement with the gift of the old chisel made Joseph smile. It would not be difficult to accommodate Abishag's request to care for her little brother.

Jezreel might be another thing. She protected her silent world from intrusion with tenacity. In the time Abishag had been gone, Jezreel had learned to graciously accept Joseph's assistance when it was required. He even caught a smile on her lips once when she watched Nathan beg Joseph to take him fishing. But it was not easy to imagine Jezreel as his wife. She was, for certain, beautiful— though not to be compared with Abishag, whose beauty had taken her from him, after all.

Joseph looked back at Abishag. She awaited his answer with a look of quiet desperation. "Do you think your father would have been agreeable to this plan?" he asked.

"I think he fretted more about Jezreel's future than anyone's," Abishag answered. "He left an inheritance that will make her life easier, and the commission Father accepted from the palace for my services will help too. Father was proud to know I would be your wife. Under the circumstances, I think he would be pleased that I would consider Jezreel's happiness before my own."

"You seem happy enough at the palace," Joseph accused quietly.

"It is an honor to be asked to serve the king." Abishag became defensive. "Father would not want me to break his commitment with the king."

"But it would have been acceptable to him to break your commitment with *me*?"

Abishag held her response for a moment. "If it is unacceptable to you to marry Jezreel, then I will fulfill my father's promise to you when my services at the palace are no longer needed." It was the only bargain she could offer Joseph.

"Perhaps Jezreel should be consulted before you trade her off." Joseph's words were calculated. The bargain would not be sealed until Jezreel's wishes were known.

"If you are not agreeable, there is no sense in bringing it up with her."

"I just want you to make this decision carefully, Abishag. If it is truly the best solution for caring for Jezreel and Nathan, then I am willing."

There was no hiding Abishag's relief. A weary sigh escaped her lips. It was not only the best solution. It was the *only* solution. Jezreel would have to accept it. Nathan would do so eagerly.

"I will talk to them this evening," she promised. "We will need to move quickly. There will be legal matters I must attend to before I return to the palace."

"Of course. A bill of divorcement is required to end our betrothal. You have thought of that?" Joseph asked as he rose to leave. He paused at the door. "Whatever must be done must be done. We cannot keep you from the king."

Abishag sat quietly in the afternoon sunlight. Joseph had insisted that she consider this decision carefully. She thought of nothing else. It had been much to ask of Joseph, but it would be sacrificial for her as well. While her residence at the palace would care for her needs at the present, a point would come when she no longer had reason to be there. Where would she go then?

She had no answer to that. There was no telling when that time would come. The king might die within days, or he might linger for months. The thought of his dying saddened Abishag. It was easier to hope that there would be many months she could spend with him. In the meantime, Joseph was in need of a wife, and Jezreel was available.

Abishag moved to stand in the archway of the kitchen. To stay busy, Jezreel was working on the evening meal. Her tangled curls were pulled back loosely and gathered at the back of her neck. Here and there, strands of the black silk strayed and dangled haphazardly around her face. Her skin glistened from the heat of the fireplace. She worked steadily, as if keeping her hands in motion would prevent her mind from thinking.

Waiting until Jezreel caught sight of her, Abishag joined her at the fireplace and placed a tender hand on her shoulder. Jezreel understood the gesture—Abishag wanted to talk to her. She stood the spoon against the edge of the boiling pot and dried her hands on her apron.

"The aroma of your supper is tempting," Abishag said, motioning toward the pot. She moved her fingertips to her nose, closing her eyes in feigned pleasure.

Jezreel shook her head. She laid her palm against her belly and turned her hand outward. Grief clung to her face.

"I understand," Abishag sympathized. "I am not really hungry either." Indeed, food had lost all taste as they mourned their father; but preparing meals was a simple part of a daily routine that would occupy their time. After all, it was time that promised to heal the hurt.

Abishag took the towel Jezreel had thrown across her shoulder. She spread it over the back of a chair. It was odd how Jezreel always worked with a towel over her shoulder. Abishag had as well. So had their mother. Even the little parts of daily life were mirrored images of their mother. Abishag touched Jezreel's elbow and motioned for her to sit. The girl seemed grateful for an excuse to rest her feet.

"You handle the kitchen chores so comfortably," Abishag praised her. "You learned quickly the tasks of this room."

Jezreel recognized the words of encouragement and smiled. As spontaneous as the smile had been, it was immediately shadowed by the sadness that had veiled her face since Eliezer's death. There was so much uncertainty in her life. Only rare occasions merited a smile now. The few smiles that dared form were brushed aside, as if happiness were an affront to her dead father.

"I need to ask a favor of you, Jezreel," Abishag said. "Please think about this before you give me your answer." Jezreel's forehead furrowed with silent questions. Abishag took Jezreel's hands in her own and spoke carefully into her eyes.

"I must return to the king, but I cannot go until I make certain that you and Nathan are cared for." Did her words sound selfish already? "You cannot stay here by yourselves. You understand that, don't you?" Jezreel's shoulders drooped, and a sigh of resignation curled one side of her lips.

"I have spoken to Joseph," Abishag continued. "If you are willing, we have agreed that you will become his bride."

The girl's eyes widened in disbelief, and Abishag knew that Jezreel had understood. She began to shake her head as she pointed to herself. She would object to the idea of Abishag breaking her betrothal, even more to the suggestion that she might take Abishag's place at the wedding. Abishag expected that, but she also knew that Jezreel must somehow be convinced to accept the plan.

"He is a good man, Jezreel," Abishag argued. "He will provide a good home for you and Nathan." A wave of relief swept across Jezreel's face at the mention of their brother's name. No doubt, she had been fretting about his situation more than her own.

"Yes," Abishag assured her, "Joseph said Nathan would be welcome to live with you. That will make you happy, won't it?"

Another sad smile whispered across Jezreel's lips. She pointed to Abishag and made a wide circle with her arm, as if to embrace the four of them together. Indeed, Jezreel would be most happy if the three siblings could be together.

Abishag shook her head. "I must return to the palace." It was not the time to explain to Jezreel that the three of them would never be together as a family again. Having requested a bill of divorcement from Joseph, it would be unseemly for Abishag to further scandalize his name.

CHAPTER 17

With the dowry already cared for, it was a simple matter of transferring to Jezreel the contents of the trousseau that Abishag had been gathering for two years. The wedding gown was hung and new sandals placed nearby to be ready for the wedding night. Though the unusual circumstances dictated that the normal period of separation be disregarded, in every other way Jezreel's marriage would be according to tradition.

Finally, the shout came in the night. Joseph and his groomsmen led the procession to Eliezer's home to claim his bride. The happy commotion stirred Eliezer's children to immediate action, and before long the enlarged wedding party was returning to Joseph's house.

Jezreel remained veiled so that no one could see her face, but Abishag sensed that the young woman was more frightened than excited about the marriage. After the vows were exchanged and the blessings had been offered, Joseph led his new wife to the bridal chamber. The appointed witnesses were secluded with the couple, and the wedding guests awaited word of the consummation.

For Abishag, the pain of those interminable minutes culminated with Joseph's joyful presentation of the un-veiled Jezreel as his wife.

But those bittersweet moments were soon blurred by the festivities of the next seven days.

Nathan pranced about during the celebration with unbridled revelry. He adored Jezreel and worshipped Joseph. How could things have turned out any better for him? His contentment with his new living arrangements was double payment for Abishag's sacrifice, and she thrilled at his pleasure.

There were few opportunities for Abishag to speak privately to Joseph. There was so much she wanted to say to him. To thank him for honorably providing for her sister and brother. To admonish him to care for them diligently. To try one more time to convince him that her heart was happy for him. When their eyes met on occasion, Abishag wanted to believe that Joseph understood the many things she longed to tell him. What he could not understand—and must not know—was that her tears flowed freely in the night solitude, painfully searing the dreams her heart had fostered of their future together. In a far corner of her soul, she erected a monument to Joseph to forever memorialize the most selfless gift he could have given her.

CHAPTER 18

THE KING HAD SENT REGULAR couriers to bring him news of Abishag. So it was that arrangements were made to bring her home to the palace. In the carriage, Abishag resolutely forbade a look behind. She had cared for things the best she could. Eliezer's fish stall had been sold. Jezreel and Nathan had chosen things from their home to complement the furnishings Joseph had provided for their new home. After that, Eliezer's house had been barred and locked, presumably for Abishag's eventual return.

Her heart fluttered with the anticipation of seeing the king. According to the couriers, his health had not deteriorated, and that news alone alleviated the loneliness she felt for him. What an odd thing, their relationship! The king surely had not languished over her absence; but in truth, he had persistently sent word from the palace and asked for news of her. That was as near to affirmation of his affection as Abishag might ever get.

She had much to report to the king upon her return. Abishag wondered if he would approve of the choices she had made to care for Jezreel and Nathan. Or would he see only that her own future had been compromised and be disappointed that she had been so shortsighted?

115

The carriage slowed to city's pace. Abishag yawned and stretched like a kitten waking from a nap. She pushed back the curtain at the small window and reacquainted herself with the busy streets of Jerusalem. It was amusing how the traffic opened a path for the king's carriage. If only the common people knew how common was the carriage's passenger!

Abishag became aware of the steady clopping of horse hoofs alongside the carriage. From her seat, she could not see the rider; but when she heard the voice, recognition gripped her heart.

"Who is this?" was the haughty inquiry.

"Abishag of Shunem is returning to the palace," came the reply.

"Indeed? I feared we had seen the last of her." The sneer on Adonijah's face was easy to imagine. He spurred his horse and took off toward the palace ahead of the carriage. All of Abishag's palace reminiscences during her absence had excluded this dark thread in the tapestry of her life. Hearing his voice revived her fears of him. Though she would be protected in the king's chambers, the king was still oblivious to the protection he provided. Better to keep it that way.

When Abishag was ushered into the king's chambers, she found Bathsheba visiting there. It was the king who saw her first. Abishag did not miss his pleased smile as he welcomed her.

"Abishag!" he called. "How good to have you back!"

Bathsheba turned to greet her. The ever-so-slight frown on Bathsheba's face reminded Abishag that she still wore the common robe from home. Part of her wished to slip behind the panels of her sleeping area and correct all the imperfections that manifested themselves most prominently in the queen's presence. But a stronger part of her wished to see the king first and ascertain for herself that he had not failed in her absence.

"Yes, welcome back," the queen added enthusiastically. "Your patient has missed your doting care." She turned her teasing smile back to the king.

"Come here, child." The king stretched out a hand to Abishag. She lay her palm against his and felt his fingers close around hers. What inexplicable comfort his touch provided! "We were saddened to hear the news of your father. It was good that your Joseph came to take you home when he did."

My Joseph? Abishag wondered. The couriers must have failed to bring word of her sister's wedding. It was understandable that a wedding in Shunem would not be noteworthy news in the palace. It would be easier to tell the king about Jezreel and Joseph when she was alone with him.

"I doubt my father knew I had come home, but it was good that I was there with Jezreel and Nathan when he passed." Abishag spoke of her father's death, still numbed by the consequences of it. "Thank you for making your carriage available for my trips. It was very kind of you."

Bathsheba stood and wrapped her arm around the girl's shoulders. "We were happy to do that for you, Abishag. We only wish we could do something now to ease your sorrow."

"I need to get back to my responsibilities," Abishag answered. "Keep me busy, and that will help as much as anything." The king squeezed her hand tenderly.

"I will let you take over now," Bathsheba said. "And in case he does not brag on himself, you should know that the king's feet have touched the floor every day since you have been gone." She leaned to kiss his cheek.

"Every day?" Abishag quizzed the king. "I'm pleased that you were not allowed to loaf in my absence."

"I think I promised you a stroll when you returned," the king bantered.

The heavy chamber doors shut firmly behind the queen. As if on cue, a deep sigh released Abishag from the pressure she often felt in the queen's presence. To be honest, Bathsheba had never been unkind. Quite the opposite. They even shared the secret of Adonijah's threats. Still, Abishag could not shake the sense of inferiority that clung to her when she stood next to the queen.

"You are weary, child," the king said. "Come and sit beside me."

"Perhaps you should show me how easily you can sit yourself up now," Abishag suggested.

"I have already been up today. Tomorrow will be soon enough to demonstrate how spry I have become." He patted the space beside him.

"Very well. I will sit for a few minutes then."

"The evening meal will be delivered soon," the king reminded her. "When you have eaten, you must go unpack and get some rest. Utter exhaustion clouds your eyes."

There was no denying her weariness, but it was so very comfortable being back in the king's chambers. Abishag felt her spirits begin to respond to his presence like a flower turning to absorb the sunshine.

The palace food did not tempt her appetite, but Abishag nibbled at it while the king enjoyed his meal. She remembered how only a few months earlier she had lifted each bite to his lips. Now, he managed his own utensils and sipped from his cup without assistance. Had she succeeded in nursing him to the point of becoming unnecessary?

It was a quiet meal between them. The king seemed to sense her need for silent companionship. When Abishag's eyes met his, she found a look of tender concern watching her carefully. It was comforting and disconcerting all at the same time. She busied herself collecting the empty dishes onto his tray.

That done, she returned to her partitioned corner and replaced her traveling items into the old trunk from home. They were things she would not need for some time, and she handled them thoughtfully as she folded them into neat piles. They were, as it were, pages from a closed chapter of her life.

She sat wearily on the edge of the soft bed, gathered the old sleeping robe close, and buried her face in its familiarity. She stood and loosened the belt of her traveling clothes and pulled the shift over her head. For a moment, she considered climbing in naked between the warm blankets of her bed. There seemed no energy now to slip into her sleeping gown; but if the king should need her in the night, she would not want to take time to fumble with her clothing.

"Before you lie down, come here again, child," the king called.

Abishag sighed inwardly. She reached for the fresh silken robe that hung in anticipation of her return. She pulled it close around her to hide the commonness of her own clothing.

"May I do something for you, my lord?" she asked as she neared the foot of his bed.

"Only this," the king replied. "Hand me my harp and ask the doorman to come to me."

Abishag lifted the gilded instrument to his waiting arms. Strange requests, both of them, but she was too tired to question him. She opened the chamber doors and whispered to the attendant. Satisfied that she had completed the king's assignments, she collapsed into the warmth of her bed.

"I want *no* interruptions the rest of this evening," she heard the king demand. "Abishag is sleeping, and I do not want her awakened." The doors closed quietly, and the king and his nurse were sealed into the ordered seclusion.

Just as Abishag's eyes closed, the soft ripple of music kissed her ears. Her eyes opened wide, and she understood the king's request for his harp. The music continued, a gentle lullaby that drifted into the secret places of her heart and soothed her aching soul. Abishag turned onto her back and closed her eyes to enjoy the sensation without distraction. The sweet notes his fingers plucked lifted her to soaring ecstasy. They then became so soft that her heart plummeted in a breath-taking freefall, only to be gathered up again on the wings of the gay music. At last, her weariness prevailed and she slipped off into sleep, still humming with the pleasure of it all.

When Abishag woke the next morning, her cheeks were cool. She pulled the soft blankets close and wiggled in great yawning stretches beneath them. Fully awakened, she blinked her eyes as she remembered she had returned to the palace. Suddenly, the odd freedom of sleeping late vanished. She sat upright to listen for movement from the king's bed.

"Goodness!" she whispered aloud. "How late can it be?" She tossed aside the blankets and worked her toes into the slippers on the floor. She shook her head to loosen the tangled curls.

"You have finally awakened?" the king teased from across the room.

"I have never slept so late," Abishag replied.

"And I have never waited so long for my breakfast," his teasing continued.

Abishag heard the playfulness in his voice. Still, tending to the king's needs was her responsibility, and she felt as if she had neglected him. "I will bring your meal in just a moment," she promised.

"You will *not*," came the immediate response. "You will enjoy your bath as usual this morning, and then we will eat together."

A tone of finality ended the conversation. Abishag slipped into her robe and gathered the hair combs she had not used since returning to Shunem. From her corner, she could see that Rachel had delivered fresh towels and robes for the day. So, it was true, and not a dream. She was back in the palace, and all the joys and fears of her existence had resumed. Abishag went to the fireplace to carry water to the bathing room.

"You know," the king commented as he watched, "I do have servants who could assist you with that."

"Your servants are not *my* servants," Abishag answered quietly.

"Oh, but they are if I wish it," the king corrected. "And I *do* wish it. From now on, you are to alert the attendant when you are ready to bathe. He will carry the water for you."

"Next, you will have the queen's attendants accompanying me to the bathing room," Abishag predicted. "Forgive me, my lord, but there are certain things I would prefer to do for myself. I can carry my own water."

"You have a stubborn independence about you," the king said. "I like it. Let's agree that you will ask for the assistance of my servants when you need it, shall we?"

"Agreed." Abishag disappeared into the bathing room with the last jar of water. She poured a few drops of the perfumed oil into the bath and breathed in deeply the sweet aroma that rose in the steam. Her robes fell to the floor at her feet, and she stepped into the water. She knelt down so that the water covered her shoulders. For a long moment, she did not move. The lateness of the hour would not allow her to prolong her bath, and soon she was sponging the water over her face and arms.

Amidst protests from the doorman, Adonijah flung open the chamber doors and swaggered into the king's rooms. He paused and looked about the room, sniffing the scent of perfume in the air. A glance towards his father's bed assured him that the king was resting. He stepped into the bathing room, pleased that Abishag's back was to him and she seemed unaware of his presence. What fortunate timing for him! The woman stood and the perfumed water dripped off her glistening skin. Anticipating her next move, Adonijah took the towel from the hook where it hung.

"Please, allow me to help you." He stepped back from the bath and offered the towel from a distance. Startled by his jeering smile, Abishag sank down into the water to cover her body.

"Get out!" she demanded in a whisper.

"I will not," came his low reply. "I am not accustomed to taking orders from someone such as you." He laughed at her predicament. "I will have you some day," he threatened in whispered words. He tossed the towel at the girl and left the room.

Adonijah approached the king's bedside. "Good morning, Father," he greeted loudly to wake the king from his sleep.

"Good morning, Adonijah," the king replied as he stretched. "What brings you here so early?"

"I am leaving for a few days to hunt with my friends," Adonijah answered. "I wanted to let you know." He tossed his head toward the bathing room. "The room is filled with the lovely smell of bath oils. How do you deny yourself the pleasure that wench could offer?"

"She is beautiful, is she not?" the king agreed with a weary smile.

"Indeed!" Adonijah concurred. "When you are finished with her, I would gladly take her for my own."

The king laughed at his son's eagerness. "She is not mine to give, Son. Besides, there is a man in Shunem who waits to wed her."

"Perhaps I can distract her," Adonijah schemed.

"Don't hope for that," the king directed. "She takes her betrothal very seriously and is looking forward to her marriage."

"Then I shall have to enjoy her while she is here with you." A sneer played at the corners of Adonijah's lips.

"Enjoy with your eyes, Son," the king admonished. "Nothing more can come of it."

"We shall see." Adonijah would not give up so easily. "Nevertheless, I will be away from the palace for a few days. I will be back to see you when I return."

Abishag trembled as she tidied the bathing room, reluctant to face the king. She was certain he had not heard Adonijah's taunts, or surely he would have put an end to his son's intrusion. Remembering the queen's wishes that the king know nothing of Adonijah's encounters with her, Abishag determined to tuck the incident away in a far corner of her mind. She pulled her wet hair up into a bundle of curls and secured them with the pearl combs.

"I have missed the smell of your bathing," the king remarked as she approached his bedside. Abishag only smiled. He did so make her feel welcome here.

"Your breakfast will be cold, I'm afraid," she said as she set the tray before him.

"It would not hurt me to miss a meal," he replied, "but surely there is some part of it that is still edible."

"I should not have lingered so over my bath," Abishag apologized.

"Nonsense. You look rested and refreshed. The time was well spent."

Abishag buttered her hard roll. It was more than her stomach wanted, but the king would notice if she did not eat. "Have you practiced the harp in my absence?"

The king looked directly into her eyes. "No. I was surprised how easily it came back to me last night."

"Your music was beautiful," Abishag responded. "It lulled me to sleep too soon. I could have enjoyed it for hours."

"I had forgotten the pleasure it brings to play," he said softly. "It pleases me that you enjoyed it as well."

"I'm sure I must have fallen asleep with a smile on my face," Abishag guessed.

"Then I will play for you again sometime."

"Soon," Abishag begged. "Perhaps we could play together. I have never done that before, but surely the music of two harps could only be twice as beautiful."

The king laughed aloud at her enthusiasm. "It seems I have found the secret passion of your heart." His laughter rose as he saw Abishag's face turn crimson. "Passion is a good thing, child. It is what keeps the soul young. You will see."

Abishag set her cup firmly on the tray. "Passion will never be a part of my life," she declared. Tears crept to the corners of her eyes.

"Of course it will," the king argued. "Your Joseph will draw it out of your heart. But it will be up to you to let him know what pleases you."

"It will never happen," Abishag repeated boldly. She stood and walked to the fireplace and busied herself with the kindling. She angrily tossed the wood into the fire. She had no future with Joseph now; and if passion was what fueled Adonijah's desires, she wanted no part of it.

"Why are you so certain?" the king asked.

Abishag turned to face him, but she kept her distance. She swallowed hard before answering. "Joseph and Jezreel were married before I returned."

Surprise silenced the king. His eyes remained fixed on Abishag's face. He seemed to be searching for answers to questions he did not want to ask. "But why?" he finally asked.

The tears that had threatened before now crested and spilled onto Abishag's cheeks. She had never faltered in making the decision to give Jezreel her place with Joseph, but neither had she allowed herself time to grieve over the end of her relationship with the man. "Because it was the best way to provide for Jezreel," she answered slowly.

"Joseph agreed to this?" the king asked. There was a glint of protective anger in his eyes now.

"Joseph has waited two years for me to be free to marry him," Abishag defended. "It is only natural that he would want to start his family."

"But I would have let you stay with him," the king whispered.

Abishag turned away from the king again. There was no question in her heart that the king would have released her from her commission if she had asked. To be honest, though, she had not wanted to be released. Her new friendship with the king had become important to her. In her mind, she understood that the king wished the very best for her, but her heart hurt at his quick offer to release her. And it confirmed her suspicion that the king returned none of her affection.

"I did not want to stay with him," she finally admitted. Would the king see behind her words and understand that she was offering her heart to him?

"What will you do?" His question was her answer.

"When you no longer need me, I will worry about it then."

"I never intended for you to sacrifice your happiness to care for me." Every word echoed genuine concern.

"I am not here only because of the commission signed with my father," Abishag answered. "I am where I want to be."

"Caring for an old man?" The king's words resounded with disbelief.

"Caring for a good friend," she corrected.

The king shook his head. "Caring for me will not give you a companion for your old age. Nor will it give you the children that every woman desires."

"Perhaps those are not my priorities," Abishag answered.

"They should be," the king declared softly. He allowed a long silence for the truth of his words to penetrate.

"Then I must disappoint you, my lord," she said simply.

A heavy sigh escaped the king's lips. There was a look of frustration on his face. "You do not disappoint me, child. It is just that your happiness is important to me."

"Right now, I am happy caring for you. Is that not enough?"

"You could have so much more."

Abishag picked up the breakfast tray and walked away from the bedside. "Even a king cannot choose what makes another person happy."

CHAPTER 19

Bathing the King was awkward after that. As fearful as Abishag was to further reveal her affection for the king, he seemed fearful to receive it. She had allowed him to become more than a patient, and he avoided opportunities for her touch to tempt his poor judgment. His rejection was raw. Abishag carried out her responsibilities with little joy.

Each afternoon, the king sat in the chair at his bedside and visited with his guests. The many exclamations over his improved health seemed to feed the motivation he needed to endure the rigors of exercise Abishag imposed upon him. He walked about his chambers some each day, but the promised stroll with Abishag had never happened.

The approaching Jubilee celebration was causing much excitement in the palace. Everyone had a favorite part they anticipated. Most of the men planned to participate in one activity or another. The prospects of seeing their king at the events kept the courts astir.

Solomon visited often, each time expressing his family's appreciation to Abishag for the excellent care she provided the king. Adonijah was a less frequent visitor. Abishag found ways to disappear behind her partitions when he was about. Unlike Solomon's praise, the jeering looks from Adonijah pronounced her no better than a common slut, a mere body to be enjoyed at some point.

Rachel continued to deliver fresh clothing and linens to Abishag. They chatted briefly each morning. Rachel asked often about her satisfaction with her accommodations. A peculiar look of pain always shadowed Abishag's smile. The two of them needed to find time to visit and perhaps talking with Rachel would ease the unhappiness that Abishag could not shake.

"This afternoon I will return, and we will go out for a walk," Rachel announced one day. "There is more to the world than the confines of these chambers. It will do you good to get some fresh air."

"I would like that," Abishag consented. At home in Shunem, her household tasks had taken her outside each day. Here, the threats of Adonijah forced her to cower close to the king's unknowing protection. More than anything, she looked forward to walking with the king in the gardens surrounding the palace.

Bathsheba's visits were full of reports of the preparation for the days of feasting that were part of the Jubilee celebration. It was no small task to organize such a variety of foods, and in quantities Abishag could not even imagine. Today, Bathsheba brought samples of the breads she had ordered. Much refining of recipes was being done, and tasting the products was a job she shared enthusiastically with the king.

"What do you think of this one?" she asked as the king rolled the sweet bread slowly with his tongue.

"I think you have a more discriminating palate than I if you can discern much difference between these," he said. "But it is your perfection with such details that has always highlighted the celebration with feasts that are not soon forgotten."

Bathsheba's eyes sparkled at the king's praise. "Abishag, when will Joseph be arriving for the celebration?"

Abishag froze in place. The king had not told Bathsheba about Joseph and Jezreel? "He will not be coming."

"But he must!" Bathsheba cried. "You have been separated too long. It would be a perfect time for him to spend some time here with you."

The king cleared his throat and quietly addressed the queen. "Joseph has obligations that will not permit him to travel to Jerusalem for the celebration." He locked eyes with Bathsheba and the slight pucker in his eyebrow begged the queen to let her questions wait.

"Well, then, he must come another time," Bathsheba finished.

Abishag's shoulders heaved with silent relief that the queen had not prodded for more information. It would not have been easy to explain fate's unusual twist of her betrothal.

Bathsheba gathered up the food she had brought and bent to kiss the king's forehead. "Tomorrow I will bring the final meat choices. Once we have selected from those, the menus will be completed. The celebration is coming soon!" She slipped out the chamber doors, her gowns rustling with her mission.

Abishag busied herself arranging the towel and supplies for the king's bath. Indeed, the celebration was coming soon. If they were to avoid the uncertainty of the king's stamina, he must venture outside the palace soon. Each outing would help strengthen him. She would suggest a walk that afternoon. She returned to the king's bedside, resolved in her plan.

"Did I handle the queen's curiosity to your satisfaction?" he asked as Abishag organized the bathing supplies.

"Certainly. I do need to explain to the queen what has happened, but it might be easier after a little while." Abishag lifted the sleeping shirt over the king's head. "Thank you for excusing Joseph's absence for me."

"If it would help, I can tell Bathsheba the rest of the story sometime when you are not here." The king placed a hand over

Abishag's, forcing a pause to the formality that had become a part of their togetherness.

"As you wish, my lord. I doubt the news will be sensational to the queen."

"Don't discount her sympathy so severely," the king admonished. "She has grown fond of you, as I have; and the news of Joseph and Jezreel will be met with sadness for you."

Abishag pulled her hand free from the king's. "Perhaps sympathy from the queen is not desired."

"It will be offered, at any rate. She would be a friend to you, if you would allow it."

"I dare say the queen has friends enough and no time to bother with problems of someone such as me." Abishag punctuated her words with finality. "Might you feel up to walking outside this morning?"

A silenced sigh curled one corner of the king's lips. "It is finally time for our stroll?" He smiled broadly at Abishag, clearly hoping to restore the carefree tone to their conversation.

"If you feel up to it," Abishag replied as she combed through the king's damp hair. The smell of lotions sweetened the air. Abishag remembered snuggling close to Nathan after his baths, breathing in the freshness of his skin. She would tuck Nathan's little head under her chin and close her eyes to enjoy the moment of the embrace. Here, she willed her touch to remain distant.

"I have a rule," the king said. "Never break a promise to a child. I promised you a stroll. I am ready if you are."

"We will go after I've put away these things." There was such a plea for happiness in his tone that Abishag could not help but respond with pleasure. She rushed about, fueled by the anticipation of taking the king out into the fresh air. She kicked off the soft slippers and urged her toes into her shoes from home. Before she returned to the king's chair, she heard Adonijah's dreaded voice announcing his appearance in the king's chambers.

"Adonijah!" the king welcomed him warmly. "We were just about to go out for a walk. Would you join us?"

"Is Bathsheba coming to escort you?" Adonijah asked.

"No," the king replied, "only Abishag is going with me. The queen has been here already and is off to finalize preparations for the celebration. You are welcome to come along."

"I might just do that," Adonijah decided quickly. Abishag's heart sank when she heard his answer.

"Wonderful!" the king exclaimed. "You can tell me about your final preparations for the chariot races." He paused, waiting for Abishag to return. "Come along, Abishag! The morning will be gone before we get outside."

Abishag stepped out from the protection of her partitions. Her heart recoiled in fright when she found Adonijah's wicked eyes playing over her body. Having escaped a reprimand from his father, Adonijah must know that she had kept their encounter a secret and would not report any further contact he might initiate.

"Adonijah has agreed to accompany us," the king explained, "in case I collapse and need to be carried back to my bed."

"We will not go so far that you might collapse," Abishag assured him. In fact, the stroll would be a very short one if she had her way. She took the king's elbow and steadied him as Adonijah's strength lifted him to his feet.

"We're off!" Adonijah cheered. The three of them exited the king's chambers, each nursing thoughts of a different kind.

The king's endurance surprised Abishag. Knowing he would not ask to turn back, Abishag watched carefully for signs of fatigue. She saw only a broad smile upon his face. How exhilarating the fresh air seemed to be for him. It had been months since he had felt the warmth of the sun on his skin.

Back in his chambers, the king settled wearily into his bed, and Adonijah left. "You know, Abishag, my son would be pleased if you participated more in his visits here," he said as Abishag positioned his pillows beneath him.

Her head jerked angrily to attention at the reference to Adonijah. "He told you that?"

"Of course, not," the king replied. "A father can sense when his son is interested in a young woman. Adonijah admires you a great deal."

Abishag busied herself at the head of the bed, just out of his sight. She was certain her face would betray the disgust she felt for the king's son. "I am the daughter of a common laborer. No doubt there are more eligible young women in the court who would be happy to catch his eye."

"But none more beautiful," the king declared. "And none with hands as gentle as yours."

Abishag shuddered at the thought of touching Adonijah. "I am still getting over the ordeal with Joseph, my lord. There is no room in my heart for another man's attention yet."

The king reached above his head and found Abishag's hand. He pulled her around to face him. "In time, the pain will be gone and you will be ready to love again. Adonijah would be a good provider."

Abishag's heart cried out. *Will the king bestow me on his son as if I am some piece of property? What if I tell him of Adonijah's threats? And I will tell the king before I consent to be handed off to Adonijah!*

"You are providing most adequately for me here," she said aloud. She tucked the blankets close as she spoke.

"Providing for you? You have a corner of a room to call your own, no title but 'nursemaid,' and no children to delight your heart. You deserve much more."

"It is not your responsibility to worry over my future," Abishag whispered. "I am content to be here with you." She both feared and hoped that her voice sounded as defiant as she felt. These chambers were her refuge. Leaving them for any reason was frightening. The idea of leaving them to be joined to Adonijah was horrifying.

"I will not always be here, child," the king admonished.

"As long as you are, I would prefer to be with you." Abishag could not lift her eyes to the king's face. The option of being sent to Adonijah prompted her unusually candid honesty.

"I will not send you away, Abishag, but please consider the opportunity there is for you with Adonijah. Your life would be comfortable, and your children would have every advantage."

"It is not my nature to be so calculating, my king. For now, I am content. Surely there is some merit to that." Abishag tucked one last corner of the blanket. "I will let you rest before the noon meal is served. After we have eaten, Rachel has asked if I might walk about the palace grounds with her, if you have no objections."

"Objections? Hardly! On the contrary, I applaud Rachel for coaxing you out from behind these walls. Take your time and enjoy the fresh air."

"Thank you, my lord."

The king's eyes closed, but a smile lingered at the corners of his lips. Abishag wondered if the smile celebrated the king's successful walk beyond the palace that morning, or if he was satisfied that he had solved the problem of Abishag's future. How disappointed he might be if he knew how he had instead threatened her happiness.

Rachel's knock came mid-afternoon. It was surprising to Abishag how much she had anticipated visiting with the woman. Abishag welcomed few people into her life, but she felt a need for someone with whom she could be totally honest, revealing even the thoughts she was certain she should not have. Rachel provided a listening heart.

"Grab your shawl," Rachel said. "The afternoon air has grown chilly."

Abishag glanced at the king, who was napping soundly and comfortably. She had at times sat close to his bed while he slept and watched his unconscious movement. It was a time when she was free to observe without being observed, and she leisurely took note of countless little details of the king's being. But today, she reached for her shawl, wrapped it around her shoulders, and hurried to enjoy Rachel's company.

"How is the king's health?" Rachel asked. "The courts are buzzing with the news that he ventured outside this morning."

"We did go for a short walk," Abishag confirmed happily. "He seems to be stronger each day. His appetite is returning, and he spends more time out of bed. It may be that my days are numbered here." She frowned, acknowledging the internal conflict between her wishes for the king's health to return and her dread of being dismissed from his service.

"What is the secret to your success with nursing him?" Rachel's question no doubt voiced the questions of many in the palace.

"There is no secret. He eats, he sleeps, he exercises, and I try to keep him warm. We talk a lot. Maybe I keep him too busy to give up and die."

"Does Bathsheba visit often?" Rachel looked away as she asked, but Abishag heard an echo of loneliness in her words. Was it the incessant loneliness for the companionship of a lover that haunted all the concubines? Loneliness . . . and the assumption that their not being called for declared them unlovable.

"She comes at least once every day, sometimes twice. The queen is very busy, though, and her visits are usually brief." Understanding to some degree Rachel's battle with jealousy, Abishag chose not to describe how the king's face brightened at the very sight of Bathsheba. Somewhere deep inside of every woman must be a longing to cause pleasure so simply for a man. How emotionally exhausting and short-lived it must be trying to please with only the titillating sensations offered with one's body!

"Tell me about your children, Rachel." Abishag searched for a topic to restore the sparkle to her friend's eyes.

"My children?" Rachel sighed heavily. "As a child at home with their own family, I suppose every little girl imagines the day she will have children and will mother them just as she was mothered. Who would understand at that age that being born beautiful might rob her of that pleasure?"

It was not difficult to imagine Rachel's youthful beauty. Unlike most of the concubines, her beauty had not been defaced with bitterness. There were wrinkles of sadness, but they did not completely hide her lingering beauty. Though she might be unaware, Rachel possessed a lovely soul that grew more beautiful as she touched lives with her kindness.

"My firstborn was a daughter. I loved her deeply, mostly because she was mine and partly because I knew that I would need to love her enough to make up for the absence of a father in her life. Shiloh was a happy child. Life made her giggle, and her eyes danced with delight." Rachel paused in her story. It appeared to Abishag that turning the next few pages of Rachel's life story would be difficult.

"Shiloh saw her father once each year, when the palace celebrated his birthday. He did ask about her when we were together. He always assured me that I need only ask for whatever the child lacked. I asked for nothing but her keep, and that was provided adequately.

"Shiloh was also cursed with beauty. She used it as if it were her only tool to win acceptance. She died two years ago from the disease of prostitutes."

Abishag closed her eyes against the excruciating sadness she had just glimpsed. What utter despair it must have caused to watch a daughter degrade herself so. And then to lose that child in whom she had invested so much love! Abishag reached out to find Rachel's hand and squeezed it gently. She could offer no sympathy, having never known such sorrow; but she could offer friendship to salve the disappointments life had delivered to Rachel.

"My next child was also a daughter, but she was born prematurely and lived only five days. The king was kind to me then and comforted me more tenderly than I could imagine he would. Sometimes when he called for me, we would sit close together and stare into the warmth of the fireplace. He seemed to know that my body was incapable of providing him pleasure at that point.

"But back then he called for me regularly, and I was soon pregnant again. Three of us delivered babies that season. I named my son Joshua. Though I could have turned him over to the palace wet nurses, I kept my baby with me at all times. He gave my life purpose—a reason to eat and sleep and get up each morning. Shiloh spoiled him blatantly. From the time Joshua was old enough to trot around on his own, he followed her everywhere. They were very close." A happier tone had returned to Rachel's voice. Surely this child had survived and had grown into a man his mother could claim proudly?

"Sons of concubines usually fare better than daughters," Rachel continued. "Good behavior is rewarded with appointments to good positions in the army. Joshua has done well in his appointment over the years. His valor alone has kept me in good standing with the king."

"Did Joshua marry?" Abishag asked.

"No. He watched Shiloh throw away her life and seemed determined to refuse himself any opportunity to get involved with a woman. There was not much example of happiness that way for him. He is content to devote his life to the army."

"Do you see him often?" Abishag's hope for Rachel's fulfillment through her children was beginning to waver.

"He comes when he can. Usually once a month or so." Rachel squeezed the hand she still held. "I am very proud of him, Abishag. He is a good man."

"Those are all of your children, then?"

"No, there is one more—another daughter. Hannah is a governess for the children of a captain in the army. She is well provided for in that capacity. She enjoys the children so much. There is a house servant she has become acquainted with. I expect to hear soon that they will marry."

"How exciting!" Abishag responded.

"I am happy for her. She will have the opportunity to raise the family I used to dream of, and she will be a good mother. I will introduce you to her sometime when she is visiting. You are very much like her."

"I look forward to meeting her."

The two women found themselves a considerable distance from the palace entrance. The gardens were brown from the cold weather, but Abishag enjoyed imagining them green and filled with the fragrance of flowers. Spring would begin the transformation soon.

Rachel stopped in their path and tugged at Abishag's hand. "Tell me, has Adonijah caused you any further trouble?"

"I have no reason to fear him now," Abishag assured her. "He visits his father and torments me with his evil sneers, but he will not dare touch me in the king's presence."

"Be careful. He will not forget your rejection. His kind pursues retaliation with all their energy."

"The queen keeps an eye on him for me. She seems determined to protect me from him, though I'm not sure why it matters to her." Abishag gave a return tug to her friend's hand, and they resumed their walking.

"Bathsheba despises Adonijah, and not without cause. He misses few chances to challenge Solomon. As you must know, Solomon is the queen's favored son. It is her wish that he be Israel's next king."

"It is also the king's wish. He grooms Solomon for the job at each visit, wisely counseling him in everyday decisions that will prepare him for the big decisions he will need to make for the best interest of our nation."

"They are quite different, aren't they—Solomon and Adonijah?" Rachel quietly mused.

"Adonijah was invited to walk with the king this morning. He talked of nothing but his inevitable victory at the chariot races. It is disgusting how focused he is on himself." Abishag noticed a bird nest in the tree next to them. "Look there, Rachel. We will be hearing the chirps of baby birds in no time."

"Indeed," Rachel agreed. Pulling the conversation back to Adonijah, she asked, "Did the queen report to the king about Adonijah's threats?"

"No, and she asked me not to tell the king."

"Why not?" Rachel asked incredulously.

"I think Bathsheba is waiting for Adonijah to hang himself with his father. She does not want to be accused of tattling on him. She knows the king well enough to realize that it does no good to attack someone he loves, however misguided that love might be. Besides, she has been kind enough to allow me to move into the king's chambers. She understands the safety it provides me."

"Is it awkward living there?" Rachel looked sideways at her friend, allowing time for an honest answer.

"Awkward?" Abishag replied. "Hardly. The king allows me my privacy. He is an old man, Rachel. He has spent all his passion on the queen. I think he just feels responsible for me somehow. Especially now."

"Why now?"

Abishag swallowed hard. It would be difficult to tell Rachel about Joseph and Jezreel, but she anticipated that Rachel would understand something about the sacrifice Abishag had made for her sister's happiness. To be honest, it would feel good—so good—to talk about it with her. The story spilled out.

"You are still young, Abishag," Rachel said. "There must be hundreds of men who would ask for you in marriage."

"How many men asked for you after you had been with the king?" The question slipped out of Abishag's mouth before she could stop it.

"But you have not slept with the king," Rachel argued. "Or have you?"

Abishag turned quickly to face Rachel. "No, I have not. And I will not. The king is not interested in me that way."

"Don't be too sure," Rachel warned. "He is accustomed to taking pleasure wherever he wishes. He is a passionate man, Abishag. Does that kind of passion ever die in a man?"

"I cannot say. I only know that he holds himself aloof even from my casual touch."

"Are you certain your touch is casual?" Rachel had a way of asking pointed questions at times.

"I cannot say about that either. The king has been kind to me and makes certain my needs are cared for. Talking with him feels natural. He knows how to draw the truth out of me so gently. We both enjoy the pleasures of music. He played his harp for me the first night I returned after my father's funeral. The music he played was so tender, and it brought an unusual peace to my soul. His comfort has become my life's ambition. His happiness is my reward." Abishag paused to consider all the emotion she had admitted. "Touching him makes my fingers tingle."

Rachel laughed at the enthusiasm that colored Abishag's words. There was no doubt Abishag had succumbed to the powerful attraction their king had brandished about carelessly all his life.

"Perhaps I should worry more about your feelings for the king than about the threats of his son. I'm not certain which might end up hurting you the most."

"Oh, Rachel! Any feelings for the king are ridiculous, I know. But how does one govern the choices her heart makes?"

"You have asked a difficult question, Abishag. If only a woman's heart could be governed by someone else with objectivity. I could list countless reasons to guard your heart from the king, but you would not see the danger through the veil of your affection."

"If I enjoy being with him, and he enjoys being with me, where is the danger in that?" Abishag voiced the question her heart asked repeatedly.

"The danger lies in wanting more." Rachel's answer was simple, yet so profound.

"I do not want more," Abishag answered.

"You will." Rachel's gaze dropped to the ground. "It will hurt—more than you can imagine—if the time comes when the king no longer enjoys being with you."

The king was still sleeping when Abishag returned to his chambers. She was exhausted. She kicked off her shoes and curled up on her bed. The vicious remarks of the concubines seemed like part of another lifetime. She was safe here, and comfortable. So comfortable that she drifted off to sleep in minutes.

The soft whisper of harp music woke her two hours later. Before fully waking, she imagined her mother was in the room, playing her harp as she had done each evening at bedtime. Eventually, Abishag realized the music flowed from the hand of the king. She closed her eyes and lay still, relishing the delight it gave her.

After a few minutes, the idea occurred to her to gather up her own harp and join the king's music. She stepped around her partitions with her harp in her arms, hesitant to intrude on the king's pleasure. He saw her hesitation and smiled an invitation for her to come ahead. His fingers paused long enough to pat the corner of his bed, marking the spot for her to sit. Abishag had stood beside the king's bed caring for him countless times, but she had never sat upon it. Somehow, it seemed a desecration for her to sit there.

"Please, sit down," the king invited, "and play. This is something I have wanted to do with you for a long time."

Abishag sat gingerly on the edge of the bed. She tried to balance the harp on one leg as usual, but her legs were still supporting most of her weight off the bed and the harp dangled awkwardly.

"Scoot over here," the king insisted, "and put your legs up on the bed. You cannot hold your harp like that."

Abishag felt like a scolded child and hurried to do as instructed. Her harp found its natural place on her lap then, and her fingers began plucking the strings, waiting for the right moment to slip into the melody the king played. For a while, she struggled to follow the tune exactly as he played it. At last, she gave up that attempt and began to pluck notes of her own that harmonized. Then, with the distinct sound of separate notes blending into a beautiful duet, Abishag felt transported to paradise. The ecstasy of the music filled her heart until she feared it would burst. How could such intense pleasure sustain itself?

Minutes later, the two ended their music simultaneously. Idled fingers clung unconsciously to the strings until the final echoes of the sweet music drifted into the far corners of the room. Abishag's gaze dropped to her knees. The king must surely have played like this with many partners. She imagined herself the most inferior.

"Beautiful!" the king declared. "The most beautiful music, you know, is not the matched tones of two voices singing the same melody but rather the close harmony of two distinct voices supporting each other. The same is true with instruments. We have just proven that. Did you enjoy it?" His brown eyes watched her carefully.

"Oh, yes!" Abishag tried to muffle her enthusiasm, but the sparkle in her eyes belied her pleasure.

"Then we shall do it again sometime," the king promised.

CHAPTER 20

AT LAST, THE JUBILEE CELEBRATION arrived. Abishag had heard so much about the event that she could scarcely sleep the night before. There was also considerable worry invested in how the king would fare the first long day. He had been walking outside the palace every day now for a month. Each day brought improvement in his stamina. Still, Abishag assigned herself the task of watching the king for signs of fatigue, and she would insist on returning him to his chambers before he exhausted himself.

Bathsheba had spent much time preparing the king's attire for the celebration. She fussed over the royal robe, smoothing away each wrinkle in its fine fabric. She oiled his sandals and polished his crown. And she announced that she would return this morning in time to assist the king with his dressing.

The queen arrived at the king's chambers during his bath. She sat in his chair at his bedside while Abishag bathed him, talking incessantly of the day's events. Abishag opened the bottle of lotion to rub into the king's arms and legs. Bathsheba stood then and suggested that she could lotion the king and free Abishag to care for other responsibilities before they left for the amphitheater. Abishag handed over the lotion with no apparent objection but with considerable grudging inside. It was, after all, a part of bathing the king, and that was *her* job.

It was not really a job, and that was more the problem. Bathing the king freed her to touch with excuse. She enjoyed the feel of his muscles against her slick palms. Now, she trudged on to other duties with a pout which, had it been noticed by the queen, would have been just cause for a reprimand.

Suddenly, the chamber doors opened and Solomon strode in. He had taken great care with his appearance this morning. There was no mistaking that this was the son of King David. Could the erosion of years have been erased, the king would have looked very much like Solomon at that age. Solomon, as Israel's next king, would escort his father to the royal box seats.

"You are looking splendid, Father," he said.

"Let us hope my good looks will get me through this day," the king replied in jest.

"It will hardly be your good looks that get you through the day," Solomon countered. "You are a toughened soldier. *That* is what will get you through the day."

"That and the close eye of Abishag," the king replied. "If I dare yawn, I will be banished to my chambers." He laughed when he saw Abishag frown at his barb.

"It is her 'close eye' that has gotten you to this point, Father. I, for one, appreciate all she has done for you."

"I get no credit for any of this?" the king asked, feigning insult.

"You have had time enough to prove yourself. This incredible improvement we see in you has occurred while Abishag has cared for you—coincidentally or not." Solomon turned to wink in Abishag's direction.

Abishag stepped into the royal family's box in the amphitheater and looked about her in awe. She had never imagined how small she could feel in such a magnificent setting. Four tiers of stone benches circled the arena. She had overheard Bathsheba mentioning to the king that the first tier would fill quickly with the priests and senators. Less wealthy people would compete for the seats higher up.

Solomon stood next to Abishag. "Stay next to Father, and he will explain what is happening," he advised Abishag privately.

"I do not want to disrupt his enjoyment of the events," she replied. "I will watch for you in the race. How will I know which chariot is yours?"

"We will be introduced in the opening procession. I cannot tell you yet which gate will be mine. We draw lots for our positions. You will be able to see the race well from here, though. Look for the chariot in the lead. That will be mine." His eyes sparkled as he laughed. Abishag had no doubt that he was prepared for the challenge.

"It is time for me to register," Solomon announced. "Father, I will do my best to maintain the honor of your chariot. Adonijah will not win easily, if he does. Enjoy the races!" He finished his farewell over his shoulder as he left for the starting gates.

Abishag watched the spectators gather. The air hummed with excited chatter. Several uniformed officers flanked the royal box. Their presence seemed to dissuade casual citizens from approaching the king, but a continual procession of important people stopped to greet him. The king bantered happily with them.

The sun was behind the royal box and helped warm the area. Abishag squinted as she looked down into the arena. She counted the starting gates. Twelve teams could compete at once. Perhaps Solomon and Adonijah would be in separate heats. More likely, the races had been arranged so that the most competitive teams would run together. Abishag realized her toes were tapping impatiently.

She was as anxious as any in the crowd to know the outcome of the race between the king's sons.

The blast of a trumpet announced the beginning of the races. The crowds hushed expectantly. An official stood on a platform in the center of the arena and faced the starting gates. When the trumpet silenced, the official raised a large, white flag high above his head and held it motionless. The cloth fluttered gently in the morning breeze. A second later, the flag swept to the feet of the official, and the chariots thundered out from the gates. Abishag stood and searched for Solomon's chariot.

"Solomon and Adonijah will not be in the first round," Bathsheba said. "Watch for them at the starting gates in the next heat."

Abishag's shoulders relaxed. There would be a brief reprieve from the tension of the king's sons' race. There were many questions she wanted to ask, but it did not seem appropriate to take either the king's or queen's attention from the competition. She would just observe and learn. She stood on tiptoe to watch the chariots round the far bend of the arena's center barrier. The horses' hooves threw up great wads of soil as they pounded around the track.

"Abishag, move over here beside me," the king shouted through the roar of the race. He motioned to an empty spot beside him, opposite the queen's. Abishag scooted next to him without taking her eyes off the race. She watched the center official drop another counter. Five of the seven laps were completed.

The charioteers spurred their teams to faster speeds. Each team vied for the position closest to the center barrier. They rounded the center posts so tightly that it looked as if their wheels would collide with the short wall. Even from a distance, Abishag could see that passions were growing intense. Fierce competitors held the reins of each chariot.

Across the arena, Abishag watched the crowd cheer the racers on to greater speeds. The noise rang in her head and excited her blood so that she could feel her heart pounding as the race neared completion. When the chariots crossed the finish line, the roar in the stands grew deafening.

"Great race!" the king shouted above the noise. He joined the hearty applause for the finished teams. "The next heat will begin in a few minutes. Solomon and Adonijah will be in it." His face flushed with pleasure, thanks enough for Abishag's efforts to assure his attendance at the race.

At last, the white flag was lowered and the starting gates tripped open. Solomon had told her to watch for the chariot in the lead. Abishag stretched up high in her seat. She could feel the blood pulsing through her wildly. *Solomon must win this race!*

"It will be close," the king predicted. "There is nothing like brotherly competition to make a good race." Bathsheba smiled wryly without turning to face the king. Abishag doubted the queen's confidence in her son could ever waver.

At the end of the third lap, Adonijah edged into the lead. The queen leaned forward and gripped the railing of the royal box. When Solomon regained the lead seconds later, she relaxed back into her seat. Was there more at stake in this race than Abishag knew? More than a mother's pride?

Solomon held his position through the next three laps, but then his brother's chariot pulled tightly against him in an attempt to force him to reign in. If Solomon pulled back at that point, the race would be surrendered to Adonijah. The two chariots careened around the track, leaving the other teams in their dust. At the last turn, Adonijah whipped his horses with vengeance. The animals surged violently to avoid the sting of leather against their hide. In their fury, chariot wheels collided. Spectators watched in horror as an axle snapped. Adonijah's chariot crashed down to the track and tumbled end over end.

Solomon did not look back. He coaxed his team onward with shouts of encouragement. Accidents such as this were not uncommon. Though the horses often were maimed and had to be destroyed, the men usually managed to survive, though some were maimed as well. Solomon would finish the race and then check on his brother.

The crowd turned their attention back to the finish line. Cheers were raised from one side of the arena to the other as the king's chariot slowed to a gradual halt ahead of the other teams. Solomon waved triumphantly and turned the reigns over to Jonathan. He ran to the outside edge of the arena to be out of the path of oncoming chariots then hurried back to where a crowd of officials had gathered around Adonijah's chariot.

"It is a shame," Solomon heard someone say. *Has my brother been killed?* He pushed his way through the small group and fell to his knees at Adonijah's side. He was covered with dirt mingling with blood, but he was alive.

"Have you come to hear me congratulate you?" Adonijah asked through gritted teeth.

"No. I have come to make certain I did not lose to a dead man." Solomon quipped. "Have they sent for a stretcher?"

"Just now," Adonijah moaned. "I had hoped to walk away from this mess, but I cannot even stand, let alone walk."

"Let me help you then." Solomon offered a hand to his brother.

In the royal box, the king waited anxiously for a sign that his son had survived. The crowd on the track split open, and the injured Adonijah waved weakly toward his father. The crowd cheered and stood to show courtesy to the wounded man as he was carried off the track with Solomon at his side.

The king sighed. Then he motioned for a courier. "Get word to Adonijah that I will send Abishag to care for him. Go, now!"

CHAPTER 21

IT WAS REPORTED TO ADONIJAH much later that Solomon had won the final race of the day. It was also reported that the king had retired to his chambers to rest before the evening's opening feast. Abishag listened numbly to the news. Her hands had gone to work immediately cleansing and wrapping Adonijah's wounds, but her heart beat savagely like a caged animal.

Adonijah had dismissed all his other attendants after they had shifted him to his bed. He had not spoken a word to Abishag, but behind the wincing pain, a look of triumph gleamed in his eyes.

"I have done all I can do," Abishag said coldly. She scrubbed her hands at length in the basin of water.

Adonijah closed his eyes and groaned in pain as he reached for her arm. "You are mistaken," he sneered. His fingers burrowed deep into her flesh. "There is much more you can do for me."

Abishag pulled back from the bedside, but his grip was firm. She snapped her arm up and down trying to break free from his hold.

"Listen, you wench!" Adonijah snapped. "I have only to call for Elan outside my door, and he will be here in seconds to encourage your cooperation. It would be better for you to do as I say."

Abishag recalled Elan's huge hands pinning her against the wall. There would be no escaping from him. She lowered her arm and stood motionlessly at the bedside.

"That is better," Adonijah jeered. "In my wounded condition, I can only look, but there will be pleasure enough in that for now. Take off your robe," he uttered slowly and very clearly.

Abishag swallowed hard. Her mind scurried for protection, but there was nowhere to run, and no one to come between this beast and her body. Nausea floundered in her stomach.

"Did you not hear me?" Adonijah's tone grew impatient.

"I will not take off my robe," Abishag answered evenly.

"If you do not, Elan will gladly take it off for you," he assured her. "And he might not be willing to just look."

Abishag's heart pounded, and her head began to spin. Her fingers fumbled with the belt around her robe and pulled it loose. She held its length in her hands, considering how it might be used in her defense. Reality convinced her that she lacked the strength to strangle this animal, and the belt dropped to the floor.

"You do so carefully prolong the anticipation for me." Angry eyes glared at Abishag, as if daring her to object further.

Abishag opened her outer robe and let it slide off her shoulders. Though her palms sweated, a chill crept over her body. She shivered, longing to pull closer the thin undergarments that were all that hindered Adonijah's wicked eyes.

"Now come here so that I can feel your soft skin." *He said he would only look. Now he demands touching!* Abishag's feet would not move. "Come here, I said!" he repeated through gritted teeth.

Tears pushed hard at her eyes, but she willed them away. This man might force her body to comply, but she would not give him the satisfaction of knowing how near she was to desperation. She shuffled closer to his outstretched hand. Close enough, Adonijah wrapped his hand roughly around her slight wrist and pulled her closer. The pain of his grip choked her. Suddenly he loosened his hand and shoved her backwards. He sneered as she staggered to regain her balance. "Go away!" he ordered and turned his back to her.

Adonijah slept after that. Abishag dressed and retreated to a corner of the room and crouched there for safety. How long would the king leave her here? Would he have the strength to come himself to inquire about his son's condition? Not likely, after the exhausting day at the celebration. The queen would not come, that was for certain. Solomon? If Solomon visited Adonijah, Abishag determined that she would somehow beg him to rescue her. Any repercussions with the king would be handled later. If she displeased him by refusing to nurse his son, so be it.

After a while, Abishag drifted off to sleep. Pained moans from across the room woke her and reminded her of her predicament. Perhaps Adonijah would forget she was in the room. To that end, she suspended breathing lest he hear her.

"Dear God!" the wounded man exclaimed. "The pain is unbearable! Someone do something!"

Abishag trembled in the darkness.

Elan heard Adonijah's cry and stepped into the room. He searched for Abishag as she crouched in the corner.

"Where did the girl go?" he asked as he neared Adonijah's bedside.

"What girl?" Adonijah asked sharply.

"The Shunamite, the girl the king sent to you. Where has she gone?"

"I do not know, but find her and have her do something for this pain!" Genuine distress clung to Adonijah's words.

Elan raised the lantern high and looked about the room. "Where are you, girl?" he demanded.

Abishag stood in the corner and moved into the light.

"Why have you let your master be so miserable? You must do something to ease his pain. Now!" He moved behind Abishag and pushed her toward the bedside.

Abishag assessed Adonijah's condition and said, "I will need my herbs."

"Then fetch them and get back here," Elan ordered. "The king will not be happy if you do not tend his son carefully."

Abishag rushed out the chamber doors and through the unfamiliar palace hallway. The hour was late. She passed no one. The lanterns barely illuminated the darkness. She looked down each corridor she crossed, hoping to find one that would lead to the king's chambers. Finally, she recognized where she was. She tipped her head quickly to acknowledge the chamber guards and pushed through the big doors. Inside, she flattened herself against the back of the doors and gasped on the breath of freedom.

As she expected, the king was sleeping. How she hoped he had not exerted himself too much at the celebration. She had expected to be here to help him to bed, and she had anticipated hearing his talk of the day's events. She was tempted to crawl up on the great bed beside him and snuggle close to the protection he would offer against anyone who would dare threaten her. Anyone, except his own son.

Instead, she hurried to her trunk behind the partitions and rummaged through her possessions until she found the wooden box of herbs. Her mother had taught her carefully about the power of herbs, how one herb could strengthen a tired heart while another would slow a racing pulse. Some were effective in masking pain while others, combined carelessly, could tighten a person's chest until he could not breathe. Abishag's hands grew clammy as she considered the idea that she held herbs that could end the life of the one who tormented her. Her mother's teaching had never entertained the possibility of using herbs toward that end.

Abishag paused before returning to the hallway. The king's breaths were steady and slow. His blankets outlined the form of his body. He rested peacefully, oblivious to her presence as well as to the danger he had assigned her. She could forgive him for that. In truth, Abishag would have forgiven the king for anything, quietly chastising herself for not understanding the motives of her little god. She hugged the box of herbs close and forced her steps back into the hallway.

When she neared Adonijah's chambers, raised voices cautioned her entering.

"How is it you plan to 'ruin' the wench?" Elan questioned, as if in reply to a threat uttered against her. "You have boasted the virginity of countless maidens in the court, but oddly there are no babes that bear your resemblance."

Abishag pressed closer to the door. She was certain they were discussing her fate. Suddenly, she heard a violent thud against a far wall in the chamber and the sound of a clay vessel crumbling to the floor.

Adonijah's angry voice ricocheted within the chamber walls. "Perhaps I will have you do the deed for me!"

"I dare say the girl would waste no time pointing the finger at me," Elan objected. "She will not make claims against the king's son, but I would not enjoy the same impunity."

"Then, what a pity if she should just disappear. Surely you could arrange that!" growled Adonijah. "What is keeping her? Did you not tell her to return immediately?"

Abishag had heard enough to twist the knot of fear in her stomach. She pushed open the doors and slipped into the chambers.

"Where have you been, girl?" Elan demanded. "Your master is in terrible pain, and you shuffle along so slowly!" Impatience heated his words.

Abishag held her tongue and moved past him. Adonijah was curled in pain, his face distorted with a wild mixture of agony and anger. The sight of the man gripped by such misery was an odd sort of revenge for Abishag. Surely, he would have no appetite for her body while in this condition.

She set the box of herbs carefully on the stand beside Adonijah's bed. The decision was still to be made which herbs she would choose. If her own welfare was all there was to be considered, she would poison the man without thought. But she must consider the king as well. Abishag recoiled at the distress she imagined it would cause the king if she proceeded with such a plan.

There was an alternative to the choices of poison or a hasty recovery—a concoction of herbs that would dull Adonijah's senses and maintain his drowsiness for several days. Perhaps that plan would buy her time to escape from this lecherous man. She selected the dried leaves and crushed them in the tiny bowl. She poured water into his silver cup and stirred the powder into it.

Aware that Elan stood guard over her shoulder, Abishag picked up the cup. "These herbs will not help unless he swallows it all. You must help by raising his head and holding his arms so that he cannot thrash at me because of its bitter taste."

Elan moved quickly and cradled Adonijah's head in the crook of his arm. What motivated this man to such tender care? It seemed impossible that Adonijah could foster voluntary affection from any person. More likely, Elan lived in constant fear for his position if so much as his appearance should displease his friend. Nevertheless, Abishag could find no pity for him. He had participated willingly enough in the threatening encounter in the hallway months earlier.

"Drink this, my lord," he said gently to Adonijah. "It will help ease your pain."

Adonijah tightened his lips against the bitter brew. "It would have been better if I had died in the arena!"

"Do not say such things!" Elan whispered. "Now, drink this. Swallow every drop." His rough hand wrapped around Abishag's and held the cup firmly against Adonijah's lips. The stench of sweat repulsed her, but she was caught between the two men until Adonijah consented to drink the mixture.

She returned the empty cup to the bedside stand, turned away from the sight of Adonijah, and gathered the packets of herbs into her box. "He will sleep now," she said numbly. "I am returning to the king."

Outside the chamber doors, she leaned against the wall, trembling with the full understanding of Adonijah's determination to do her harm.

Abishag opened the king's chamber doors and stood motionless just inside until she determined the king was still sleeping. Certain that he was oblivious to her return, she hurried to her bed and fell into its softness with exhaustion. She buried her face in her pillow to muffle the sobs of relief that broke free. Her skin crawled at the thought of Adonijah's hand bruising her skin.

"Is that you, Abishag?" the king's voice called softly.

Abishag bolted upright on her bed and abruptly hushed her sobs. "Yes, my lord," she answered.

"Have you come from my son's chambers? What is his condition? Should you not stay through the night with him?" The king's questions tumbled upon each other.

"I have come from there, yes," Abishag said. "Your son will certainly survive, though there will be days ahead when the stiffness and pain will make him wish he had not. He is sleeping now, and there is nothing more I can do for him."

A pause delayed the king's reply. "Must we talk through your partitions? Would you come here and visit with me face to face?"

Abishag would need hours to sooth her mind from the unexpected twists in the day's events. She could not be certain that her face would not betray her. She struggled to untangle her feet from the skirt of her robe and swiped a hand through her disheveled hair. Tired feet touched the coldness of the floor.

"Why are you still awake, my lord?" she asked as she neared his bedside.

The king held out a hand and pulled her closer when she placed her palm against his. There was a tender smile arching his lips. "I think I have grown accustomed to sleeping with the sound of your breathing, but you have not been here." He laughed aloud at the thought of a king's contentment being dependent upon the breaths of such a child. "And I have been anxious to hear about Adonijah, of course."

"Of course," Abishag agreed. What an urge she had to spit at the very sound of Adonijah's name! She would need to guard her tongue's report. "As I said, he is sleeping now. I mixed some herbs that should tranquilize him and keep him sleeping for several hours. That will allow his body time to begin healing without the hindrance of unnecessary movement."

The king squeezed her hand. "I am grateful for the care you have given him. How could I not offer your services to him, knowing there is no better care given in all of Jerusalem?"

"You speak too highly of me, my lord," Abishag cautioned.

"No, I speak from my heart," he assured her.

"How did you fare from the day's activities?" she steered the conversation away from Adonijah.

"It was a delightful opportunity I had not hoped to enjoy a few months ago," he answered. "But I must admit—to you, especially—that I am very weary at this hour. Tired, but happy that I was able to be out among the festivities. I have you to thank for that."

"I only issued the challenge," Abishag objected. The king's smile was contagious, and she found herself returning it without effort. "It pleases me that you enjoyed yourself today."

"It is unfortunate that Adonijah's accident prevented you from enjoying more of the celebration. Perhaps in a couple days he will feel up to attending the activities again, and you will not be needed. Then you must come back and sit with the queen and me."

So, she would be expected to remain at Adonijah's bedside for a while yet. She took a deep breath to smother her disappointment and turned her back to the king. He might even send her back to his son to spend the night. There would be no sleep for her there.

"I look forward to it," she replied as she busied herself refolding the blanket at the foot of his bed. "Now, you need your rest. Is there anything I can do for you?"

The king's eyes were heavy. "No. Just bring me word in the morning about my son." Abishag waited for the familiar sound of his sleeping breaths then tiptoed to the doors and marched her reluctant heart back to Adonijah's chambers.

The lamps were burning low when she slipped into Adonijah's room, but she could see Elan slumped in a chair at the bedside. Anxious to avoid waking either of them, Abishag crept quietly to the corner and spread a bed of blankets on the floor. When her mother lay dying, Abishag had learned to sob silently to relieve her heart without distressing her family. Silent sobs ravaged her now. She pulled her knees up to her chest and cocooned herself with her arms.

For the first time, she found herself longing for the simple accommodations of her home in Shunem. She had not allowed many thoughts of Jezreel and Joseph, but the remembrance of their dear faces now helped her mind escape the confines of Adonijah's room. And Nathan! How she would love to pull his wiggling body close to her and hold him tightly while she breathed in the little-boy smell. More than anything, she missed the soothing comfort of her mother's harp.

Elan mumbled noisily and shifted positions in the chair. Adonijah's sleep was undisturbed, and for that Abishag was thankful. The herbs had worked their magic. Still, he would rouse eventually and demand her attention. The more improved his condition, the more demeaning his demands would become. Abishag tried not to imagine what he might demand next. Exhausted, she finally lay down and allowed her eyes to close.

"If that wench has sneaked out of here, I'll make her pay!" Anger seethed from Adonijah's words.

Elan roused as Adonijah thrashed in his bed. "I sent her back to the king's chambers when you had gone to sleep. There seemed nothing more she could do here."

"There's plenty for her to do now," Adonijah roared. "Find her!"

Abishag had wakened at the commotion and reckoned it better to announce her presence than cause further agitation. "I am here," she said, barely disguising her contempt for her assignment to the man's care.

"Fetch some warm water and wash these wounds," Adonijah snapped.

Bathing Adonijah was unavoidable. She hung a pot of water at the fireplace and found a fresh towel. She looked for the chamber pot and shoved it with her foot toward Elan. He sent a glowering look in her direction but stooped to lift the pot and assisted Adonijah with the inferred task. Abishag turned her back and shuddered. The noise of his urine was loathsome.

When steam rose from the heated water, she poured a basinful and resolutely approached the bedside. For a brief moment, her defiant eyes lifted to Adonijah's sneering face. There would be no mistaking her displeasure in bathing him. She wrung out her cloth and washed his forehead. Her fingers prickled with repulsion at the touch of him. When she wiped his face, she tried to ignore the steely gray eyes measuring her every movement.

"Perhaps you could imagine that I am the king," Adonijah whispered crudely, "then your assignment here might be more palatable."

Abishag ignored the comment and began washing the man's chest. There were wounds to deal with here, and she concentrated on caring for them. They would require dressing changes for several days yet. Her assignment here was beginning to feel interminable.

"Augh!" Adonijah cursed when the cloth touched a raw spot.

"The wounds must be cleaned," Abishag insisted. "If you prefer that someone else do this for you, I will make way." If only there was someone else who could be charged with caring for this man!

"You have been sent to care for my wounds," Adonijah reminded her harshly.

"I *am* caring for them, though not to your liking it seems." Her voice was even and cool.

"You delight in my pain."

"I delight in no one's pain." Abishag paused her hands and stared full in his face. "But what reason have I to treat you gently?"

"You are no more than a peasant girl." There was a haughty tone to his voice.

"I have been thought good enough to care for your father, and he is the king."

"If you think you are earning favor with him, you are a fool. He has had a legion of women who have fancied themselves important to him. How many of them do you see in his company now?" He paused. "Only Bathsheba. It is always only Bathsheba."

It was true. The king called for no other woman. The concubines' quarters were filled with women who had been a favorite at one point or another. Indeed, why should she enjoy any favor with the king?

"I would not seek the kind of favor you suggest," Abishag answered. "A simple friendship with the king is by far sweeter than the fiery passions that rule his son."

"Believe what you will, but don't be surprised when your touch no longer provides pleasure and you are dismissed from the king's chambers." He laughed at his cruel prediction.

"I do not provide the king the sort of pleasure you imply," Abishag said defensively.

Adonijah snorted in disbelief. "What a waste, if that is true."

"A waste of what?" she demanded. "To force a woman's body and then discard her as violated? *That* is a waste."

"One day I will show you the meaning of violated."

He had the last word. Abishag did not respond to his threat. She might temporarily salve her fears with Adonijah's incapacitating wounds, but it was not difficult to imagine that he could enjoy inflicting pain on a body he could easily overpower.

She felt Adonijah's eyes on her every movement. How could the touch of one man bring such ecstasy while any physical contact with another repulsed her so thoroughly? Each time she wrung out her cloth, she scrubbed her hands savagely.

The chamber doors opened abruptly. Solomon strode in addressing the attendant over his shoulder. "Adonijah will see me. I won't stay long."

"Ah, Solomon!" Adonijah acknowledged his presence. "You have come to gloat over my misfortune?"

"No. I have come to make certain you are not mistreating Abishag." Solomon tossed a wide grin in her direction. He teased easily about a circumstance he presumed to be unlikely.

Abishag kept her hands busy at her task. What parts of the bath she could finish while Solomon was there would be done without comment from Adonijah. That was sufficient motivation to move along. Adonijah seemed unconcerned about being undressed in his brother's presence.

"How could someone in my condition mistreat a woman?" Adonijah exaggerated his agony.

"How indeed," Solomon bantered. "I have seen your way with women. The more they object, the more you persist."

Adonijah snorted. "You presume this girl would object to me?"

"I do," Solomon admitted. "She is not as free with her favors as you like your women. Besides, I think there is a man who already occupies her heart." He looked sideways at Abishag, measuring her response. There was none. Abishag pretended to ignore the conversation altogether.

"She is saving herself for the king," Adonijah accused.

"Don't be ridiculous," Solomon retorted. "An old man is incapable of satisfying the needs of someone so young." They chuckled knowingly.

Abishag listened to their exchange, amazed how they talked as if she were not present. *How cocky young men can be!* It would be gratifying to point out to them how the eager ineptness of young men was appreciably improved upon by the learned gentleness of old men, but they would have no regard for her opinion.

"What became of my horses?" Adonijah sobered the conversation with a question that had been begging an answer for hours.

Solomon sighed heavily before responding. "One was killed outright. The other had to be destroyed."

Adonijah swore, and his body stiffened with anger.

"Horses are replaceable," Solomon reminded him. "And men can be repaired by the likes of young Abishag. So, no need to be distressed. You will be out harassing the world again in no time." He laughed again.

Abishag rubbed lotion into Adonijah's legs and finished up the bath. How unfortunate that she had to be responsible for repairing this bit of human flesh! She gathered up the bathing supplies. It seemed a good opportunity to dismiss herself without objection from Adonijah. "I am returning to the king's chambers. You will find me there if a need arises."

CHAPTER 22

THE KING'S CHAMBERS WERE DESERTED when she returned—a good sign that he had rested well enough the night before to attend more of the Jubilee celebration activities. A strange emptiness echoed through the chambers. Abishag tumbled onto her bed. As exhausted as she was, her mind refused to stop reviewing the past day's events. In the privacy of her partitions, she remembered the pinching grip of Adonijah's hands. She covered her face with her hands as if to block out the memory of the sneer on his face. The sobs that had been stifled before gushed down her cheeks.

Weariness degenerated into self pity as her thoughts returned to the king. Though it pleased her that he felt strong enough to enjoy another day at the festivities, a part of her resented the fact that he managed so well without her at his side. Bathsheba would be with him, no doubt; and when the queen was present, Abishag imagined that she was no more than an extraneous part of the background. Always it seemed as if she were wishing the king happiness in ways that could not include her. Sleep finally overpowered her thoughts.

"Abishag? Are you here?" Rachel's soft voice coaxed Abishag out of a restless sleep.

"I'm here. Come in, Rachel." It was good to hear Rachel's familiar voice. Yesterday, Abishag would have considered it a miracle sent from God if Rachel had intervened in Adonijah's chambers.

"Why are you here alone?"

"The king is attending the festivities." Loneliness shadowed Abishag's words.

"Without you?" Rachel questioned.

"The queen is with him."

"But will she be too occupied to notice if he becomes weary?" Rachel's fear was Abishag's as well.

"He can speak for himself, but he is rather stubborn about giving up," Abishag admitted. "It is easier for him to be banished to his chambers by order of someone else."

"Were you not invited to accompany him?"

Abishag sighed. "After Adonijah's wreck at the chariot races, I was sent to care for him."

Rachel's eyes grew wide as the impact of Abishag's predicament became clear to her. "Who sent you to him?"

"The king. He still is unaware of the incident in the hallway. He believed he was making a loving gesture by sending his nurse to care for his son."

"Perhaps it is time for him to hear about Adonijah's antics," Rachel suggested angrily.

"He will not hear it from me," Abishag vowed.

"Why not? It is clear that the king is fond enough of you that he would not want any man taking advantage of you."

"But Adonijah is his son, and a father does not want to believe ill about his own son. I am not anxious to force the king to choose between his son or me. His choice would be predictable."

"Don't be too sure. It might be better to confide in him now than to wait for that despicable man to molest you—and then have the king find out." There was a ring of logic to Rachel's words. "I suppose Adonijah is harmless enough now, though."

Abishag bit her tongue against telling Rachel how Adonijah had forced her to disrobe before him and how his groping hands had touched her. Had Rachel been aware of that misbehavior, she might go to the king herself. It would be best to avoid that.

"Harmless or not, I despise being in his presence." Abishag nearly spat the words.

"As would any decent woman," Rachel agreed. "There are women, though, who would tolerate his character in exchange for the advantages he might have to offer them."

"They deserve what they get then," Abishag said with distaste.

"But what they get might not be what they expected from Adonijah."

Rachel tilted her head. "What do you mean?"

"It is just that he seems to have unusual appetites for physical pleasure." She would be vague but honest.

"Do you have to go back to his chambers?" Rachel's eyes glistened with tender compassion for Abishag's situation.

"He will use his injuries to keep me available as long as he can get away with it. I have been mixing some herbs that make him drowsy though, so he sleeps a great deal." A sly smile crept across her lips.

"How clever!" Rachel cheered her friend's self defense.

"Clever indeed," Abishag agreed, "but I cannot keep it up forever. Perhaps the king will venture to his son's chambers and see for himself that Adonijah no longer needs my services."

"The king is distracted by all the festivities," Rachel sympathized. "Hopefully, you will escape Adonijah's touch until the celebration is over and the king realizes that you are still tending to his son."

"Hopefully." But a thread of despair wound through Abishag's heart.

CHAPTER 23

Adonijah had sent an attendant to summon Abishag to his chambers. She breathed a deep sigh and headed out the big doors. Just as she pushed against them, she felt them being pulled open from the outside.

"Abishag!" the king exclaimed. "I did not expect to find you here."

Abishag stepped back to avoid a collision with the king and Bathsheba. "I was just leaving." She dipped her head and started to move around them.

"Not so quickly," the king said, slowing her down with an outstretched arm. "Tell me how Adonijah is faring today."

"He has been resting well, but he will need to exercise soon, before his muscles stiffen."

"There is none better than you to assist him with that,' the king proclaimed.

Abishag's heart sank. The king expected her to nurse Adonijah to a full recovery before inviting her back to his chambers. "Whatever pleases you, my lord." She feared her words would betray her disappointment. She could not bring her eyes to meet Bathsheba's.

"Perhaps you should visit your son and see for yourself how he is improving." The queen's suggestion was issued like an order.

"I shall do that." The king smiled broadly at Abishag.

"Your son would enjoy a visit very much, I'm sure." Abishag struggled to keep her voice natural. "I must go now. Adonijah is not a patient man." She slipped past the king and out the doors. How she wished she could have been the one holding his arm so carefully. She would have settled him down in the comfort of his bed and begged him to tell her every detail of his day. Instead, it was Bathsheba who ushered him to his bedside.

Abishag hurried through the corridors to Adonijah's quarters. The attendant had made her return sound urgent, though she doubted any real emergency warranted such concern. The doorman was not at his post when she arrived, so she knocked lightly and waited for an answer.

"Who is there?" a low voice snarled.

"It is Abishag."

"Finally!" Adonijah shouted. "Get in here, and close the door behind you."

Abishag stepped into the dark room. A strange quietness alerted Abishag to the threat of being alone with Adonijah. She closed the door and leaned against it, her feet as unwilling to go near the bedside as her frightened heart.

"You need not barricade the door. No one will try to get in." Adonijah laughed.

Abishag moved away from the door. She would disguise her fear as long as possible. "The message was sent that I was needed here. What is it you need?" She forced confidence into her words as well.

"Need you? Hardly! There are a dozen women who would fight you for this chance to be alone with me. I have only to ask for any one of them. But you? It is what you have that I want." He relished the frightened eyes that hid beneath Abishag's black lashes.

"Then you are feeling much improved?" Abishag asked. "The king will be delighted to hear that report when I return to his chambers shortly."

"You will have much to report to him when you return, indeed!" Again he laughed viciously. "I wish you to bathe me." Mischief danced in his eyes.

Abishag swallowed the knot that had formed in her throat. "I bathed you this morning. There is no need to do it again."

"Perhaps not, but I so enjoyed it that I wish you to repeat it." His haughty look dared her to deny him.

"As you wish." Abishag gathered the bathing supplies. There was no water warmed for a bath at this time of the day, so she filled a heavy pot and placed it over the fire. Heating the water would buy her a little time to settle her nerves. Perhaps someone would chance upon them and prevent his misbehavior.

"Your father plans to visit you soon to see for himself how you are doing. When he sees how much improved you are, he might wonder why you still require my attention." Abishag hoped to plant a seed of caution in Adonijah's mind.

"Really!" Adonijah's tone did not shake. "If he comes soon enough, perhaps he will witness how truly fit I am."

Abishag shuddered at his inference. "Where is Elan? Are you certain you would not need his muscles to assist you in your pleasure taking?" She looked boldly at the wounded man who threatened her.

"Elan?" Adonijah snickered. "I sent him on an extended errand. Besides, he knows me well enough to give me privacy when I want it."

"Oh, he no doubt knows your methods very well." There was an air of confrontation in her voice.

Adonijah turned to look squarely into her eyes. "Princes need much diversion to keep us happy. Elan is merely a diversion for me. You need not fear that he is my only interest."

"Such a pity," Abishag said dryly. "He seems so fond of you. I wonder, does he know he is merely a diversion for you?"

"Who can say?" There was no compassion in his words. "What Elan does know is that I have intended to ravage your body since the first day I met you. Though he would enjoy participating, he was agreeable enough to run my errand." An evil smile crept across his lips.

"There are some in the palace who would advise you not to touch me." Abishag's threat was delivered slowly and deliberately.

"So, you are a protected little bird?" Sarcastic laughter ricocheted from the chamber walls.

"Perhaps not at the moment, but be assured there have been some promises made regarding your well-being in the event you put a hand on me."

"Will you run and tell my father?" He paused for her answer. "I think not. You chose to keep our encounter in the hallway a secret between us. And why? Because you know my father would not see the offense in my enjoying your goods. It is a normal thing for a man to take pleasure in a woman's body. Father would only cheer me on—and consider you fortunate for being so favored by his son."

Abishag's confidence faltered. Adonijah was correct. His father would think it a good opportunity for her to be well cared for by someone with Adonijah's status. And, if the room full of concubines were any proof, King David could not deny the pleasures he himself had known with countless women.

"Good! I see that you understand my position. Shall we proceed with the bath?" He raised his eyebrows, silently commanding Abishag to begin.

She poured steaming water into a basin and carried it to his bedside. She wrung out the cloth and wiped his face mechanically. Pulling back the cloth of his sleeping gown, she washed his neck.

Suddenly, he raised his hand and captured hers against his skin, holding her hand in place.

"There is no need for modesty. Look about. Do you see anyone watching?" He grabbed her wrist with one hand and reached to untie her robe with his free hand.

Abishag stepped back from him and clutched at her clothing. She twisted her arm angrily to free her hand from his, but his grip only tightened.

"I am not opposed to ripping your clothing off, if that is what you wish." Anger spiced his words.

"I am opposed to breathing the same air you breathe," Abishag retorted.

"Ah! What spirit you possess!" Adonijah pulled her close to the bedside and yanked her robe down from her shoulder. The cloth cut into her neck, and she heard the sound of fibers tearing. His big fingers snatched at her underclothing so forcefully that her shoulders were uncovered in one movement. His free hand went to the back of her neck, and he pulled her down to him. He bit savagely at her lips.

Abishag arched her neck to pull her face away from him. Adonijah quickly entwined his fingers in her loose hair and pulled it like reins until she could not move her head. She could feel her scalp stretch back from her forehead; tears blurred her vision.

"Why must you struggle so?" he whispered.

Abishag sealed her lips resolutely. She would give him no satisfaction by admitting the fear that possessed her. Frustrated, Adonijah turned her loose and shoved her away from his bedside. She stumbled backwards and grabbed for the table to steady herself. Water splashed from the basin and dampened her robe. "Get on with the bath!" he barked.

Abishag turned her back to him and straightened the tray of bathing supplies. She reached to pull her robe back into place, but the tear was too long and the fabric gaped loosely at her neck. She squeezed the cloth and turned back to Adonijah.

When the bath was finished, Abishag quickly escaped out the chamber doors. Elan was waiting in the outer chambers. His eyes did not miss Abishag's torn bodice. Rage crimsoned his face, and Abishag feared she would be abused at his hand next. Instead, he pushed past her and angrily slammed the chamber doors behind him.

Elan made no attempt to muffle his words. "What is there about that wench that excites you so?" His incensed words sizzled with jealousy.

"Don't be ridiculous!" Adonijah hissed. "All I want from her is her virginity so that—just once—I can spoil something my father will withhold from me and bequeath to Solomon."

"What do you care if Solomon gets her?" Elan's words were now iced with hurt. "What do you care about *any* woman?"

"Take care, Elan," Adonijah cautioned. "Your jealousy is showing."

Abishag could listen no more. She pulled her robe tightly around her and hurried for the security of the king's chambers. Elan might well be the more dangerous threat to her if he sought to revenge Adonijah's betrayal at her expense.

CHAPTER 24

J UST AS SHE ARRIVED AT the king's chambers, Abishag saw Rachel coming down the corridor with fresh linens for the next morning's baths. The sight of her was calming.

"Abishag!" her friend exclaimed. "Whatever happened to your robe?"

Abishag had forgotten how disheveled she must look with the ripped robe. She reached up and pulled the tear together to cover her undergarments. She had not thought ahead how she would explain the robe to the king, or to Rachel. No logical explanation came to mind to offer either of them.

"You have been with Adonijah, have you not?" Rachel was clearly piecing the story together one thought at a time. Abishag bowed her head and refused to meet her friend's piercing eyes. "Did he do this to you?"

Abishag could not speak.

Rachel grabbed Abishag at the shoulders and gently shook her. "Abishag, tell me what has happened. You cannot deny that the animal has attacked you."

From somewhere deep within her soul, Abishag mustered clarity of mind to plot a solution to her predicament. "Rachel, you must come with me to the king's chambers. In case he is awake, you must chatter with me from the doorway until I reach my partitions, and so distract the king from noticing me. I will change into the robe you brought for tomorrow. You must take this robe and destroy it." Abishag waited for Rachel to comprehend her part in the deception. "Will you do that for me, Rachel?"

"Abishag, can't you see how important it is for you to tell the king about Adonijah's behavior? You cannot let this continue." There was such tender urgency in Rachel's words.

"Not yet, my friend," Abishag begged. "When there are others about, Adonijah feigns great handicap. Who would believe my stories how one so maimed could overpower me as he does? His father, least of all! No. It would be assumed that I had sought Adonijah's attention, and I did not."

"You ask me to wait until some harm is done to you before I report his behavior to the king? Please do not ask me to maintain silence about this."

"But I *do* ask it of you, for a while longer. If I tell you why, you must swear to secrecy." Abishag whispered now, fearful of the power the secret might wield.

"Secrecy?" Rachel looked perplexed.

"Yes. Hear me out. I do not believe Adonijah will ever molest me. He might threaten me as he did this evening, but he will not violate my body."

"How can you be so sure?"

"Because . . . he is incapable." Abishag uttered her answer slowly, hoping Rachel would understand what she was suggesting.

Comprehension washed across Rachel's face, followed by pure disgust. "How can you know this?"

"It is true. I overheard Elan reminding Adonijah that his boasts of conquests were unfounded."

"Then why does Adonijah chase after you?"

"He wants only to spoil me before his father gives me to Solomon."

"Do you expect to be given to Solomon?"

Abishag shook her head. "Why would Solomon want me? I am a Shunamite peasant. He is going to be our king."

"That does not answer my question. I asked if you expect to be given to Solomon?" Rachel pressed for her answer.

"The king has never suggested such a thing. Why would he? Solomon's marriage will be a political arrangement with some ally. I have nothing like that to offer the royal family."

"Be careful, Abishag. You forget that royalty does not live like common people. Concubines will be collected for young Solomon. Perhaps that is what Adonijah sees as your fate."

Concubine? Abishag's heart plummeted. She had never considered the possibility of belonging to a man in any capacity but as wife, and an only wife at that. The idea of being no more than a pleasure toy made her stomach turn. From what she had witnessed of concubine life, it surely could be no worse to never marry and live destitute for lack of a provider.

If the king were willing to give her away to his son for that use, she would be certain he had no affection for her at all. Indeed, had he been young enough to need the pleasures her body might afford, perhaps he would have used her to that end himself. A giant knot of disappointment pounded in her heart.

"I will be no man's concubine," she announced.

"Abishag, my dear friend, in the end you will be whatever the king asks of you. Because he is king, but also because you have sold out your heart to him. Pleasing him has become more important to you than breathing."

How did this woman know her heart so perfectly? Was Abishag gazing into a mirror and seeing in Rachel what her own life would be like in twenty years? Did Rachel still have so tender a spot for her king? If so, how could she befriend another who also loved the king? *Indeed, how does one learn contentment in sharing the affections of a man?*

Rachel had finally consented to take the torn robe and dispose of it in the palace garbage, to be burned the next morning. Abishag removed it and wrapped it carefully in a towel. It was not time to confront the king about his son's behavior; and if Bathsheba saw the robe, she might confiscate it as proof that Solomon was a better man than Adonijah. Solomon was, without question, the better man, but Abishag was not interested in having her virtue questioned as a result of such a show of character.

The king had not returned from the Jubilee festivities, so Abishag ventured around her partitions and approached the great bed on tiptoe. She laid her hand on the heavy spread. It had been pulled smooth by the chamber attendants. Even his pillows were fluffed and ready for his return. With no task to occupy her hands, she wandered around the empty room, anxious for the king's company. Finally, she settled down on the step next to the king's harp. She pulled her knees up to her chin and wrapped her arms around her legs.

From there, Abishag let her eyes caress the gilded instrument. She had once plucked the strings on the king's harp. It seemed so long ago when the queen first introduced her to the king's chambers and she had played his harp for him on command. Now, she would not allow her fingers to touch the fine instrument even in his absence. Her awe of the king had extended to his possessions, but she found some pleasure in mere proximity to his belongings. How he would shake his head at her minor ecstasies!

It was easier to discount Adonijah's threats when she was in the safety of these chambers. He had not, after all, done her any real harm; and her logic for no longer fearing a sexual assault seemed flawless to her at this distance. She was not so sure about Elan. It was clear that his jealousy colored his self-control. It would be wise to keep an eye out for him.

"Whatever are you doing down there, Abishag?"

The king's voice wakened her. She pulled away from the foot of the bed and stood to greet him. "I guess I dropped off to sleep, my lord," she apologized.

"If your bed is uncomfortable, you might have rested on mine," he replied with a smile.

"I have a fine bed," Abishag countered quietly. "I was waiting here for you to return."

"Here we are!" Bathsheba replied gaily as she ushered the king to his bedside chair. "This old soldier was beginning to wear me out. It was time to bring him home."

"Wear *you* out? Impossible!" The king collapsed in his chair and leaned back wearily. "What a grand day it has been!"

Abishag brightened at his good humor. Perhaps he would have stories to share with her. They would not be shared over their evening meal, however. The king had enjoyed the palace feast with his queen, and Bathsheba seemed in no hurry to leave them alone now. She had pulled up the guest chair next to the king's and settled into it. Abishag shuffled back behind her partitions as the two of them revisited the day's adventures.

"Surely, Solomon will win the final chariot race tomorrow," his mother predicted.

"Without a doubt," the king agreed happily. "Tomorrow there will be many grand prizes awarded. I expect Solomon to bring home his share."

"It has been wonderful to have you with me at the festivities," Bathsheba said. "I did not expect you to be able."

"You had given me up for dead, had you not?" There was laughter in his words. Abishag knew there must be sparkles of mischief in his eyes as well. "If I had given you up for dead, what point was there in finding such a capable nurse for you? It will be difficult enough for me to let you go when I must. I am not anxious to let you die just yet." There was no mistaking the sincerity of the queen's affection.

"It might be that Abishag has rescued me from the grave for now." The king's teasing continued. "There is new energy that pumps through my blood, but there will be an end to it eventually. I have not forgotten how weary I had become of breathing. It will happen again, and then you must let me go."

Their conversation had stumbled upon a subject Abishag would rather ignore. It was impossible to imagine life without the king. Like a child, she covered her ears with her palms, as if not hearing talk of his death would prevent its happening. She had in the past made bargains with God to spare her loved ones, but to no avail. It seemed unlikely God would now honor her selfish request for the king's life.

"It will be easier for me, knowing that Solomon has your blessing as the new king." Bathsheba's words grew soft.

"He has my blessing, as well as God's, my dear." He took her hand and enclosed it between his own. "Solomon has given your life much joy. God was good to give us another child such as him. There were times when I feared you would wither away with grief for our first child."

"Those days were my blackest. I saw nothing of love in God's dealing with us then. Only punishment."

There was a long silence. Abishag could only imagine the depth of emotion the king and Bathsheba had shared at that time. There were, it seemed, painful memories that forged their friendship to a strength she would never know with the king.

"God loves us in ways we cannot understand," the king replied. "It is not His way to muscle us into obeying Him. The misfortune we sometimes view as punishment is really just the natural result of our poor judgment; but it is easier for us to claim mistreatment than to admit to poor judgment."

"You are right, of course," the queen agreed.

Abishag listened to the king's words, awed by his wisdom, and thought the queen's reply too casual. Did Bathsheba understand the beauty of the gem she possessed in the king? Or were his qualities those that needed a certain distance to fully appreciate?

"It seems Solomon should be selecting a wife soon." How like the king to steer the conversation along an easier path. "Has he shown a special interest in any young woman?"

"He shows an interest in nearly every beautiful woman," the queen replied with soft laughter. "Perhaps he needs guidance from his father in making a choice."

"A father's guidance in those matters is seldom welcomed," the king remarked. "But perhaps there are ways that he could be encouraged to choose as we would. Surely his mother has decided whom she would choose for him."

"Solomon is like his father in many ways. Like his father, he knows his own mind. I doubt there would be much point in encouraging someone who does not naturally interest him."

"Then we must trust his judgment and his timing," the king advised.

"There might be less appropriate possibilities he wishes to consider. Goodness knows, there are a host of young women who would like to be considered. He may well have his harem gathered before he chooses a wife."

"Experience often makes a better husband," the king said.

"That experience usually results in a collection of broken hearts," the queen countered. "A collection that most men handle rather carelessly."

"So it must seem to women. Still, though we are such inconsiderate creatures, women accept our attention willingly." For a moment, he paused to enjoy the queen's exasperation. Then he laughed heartily. "Indeed. God has designed us to need you, in spite of yourselves," the queen countered. Again the king chuckled loudly. Abishag listened with a smile. Hearing his laughter offered assurance that everything was right with the world. "Don't you find it interesting how a man's 'experience' is to his benefit, but a woman with similar 'experience' is unworthy of marriage?"

"You question nature itself, Bathsheba. I have no solution to the inequity you pose." He patted her knee affectionately. "And you cannot assign yourself the task of managing all human behavior."

"I will exert influence where I may, then," the queen replied. "For now, it is time for you to rest. I will leave you in Abishag's care." She stood and leaned to kiss the king tenderly.

Abishag waited for the king to call her. It was awkward listening to the king's conversations and trying to be oblivious of the content. Her heart would have sent her rushing around the partitions and into his presence as soon as the queen left, but sometimes it felt better to be invited to join him.

"Have you fallen asleep behind there?" he finally asked.

Abishag climbed down from her bed and shook out the tangles in her robe. She patted loose hairs back into place and chased her thoughts back to the task of caring for the king.

"Are you ready for me to help you into bed?" she asked.

"In a while," the king replied. "Right now I would enjoy playing our harps together. Would you like that?"

The smile that washed across Abishag's face gave the king his answer. "Oh, yes! Let me hand yours up and then I will get my own." Her feet scarcely touched the floor in her delight. She hurried back with her harp cradled in an arm and settled down on the step at the king's feet.

"What tempo shall we play?" the king asked. "Playful? Relaxed? Serious? You pick it." He smiled as he watched Abishag consider her response.

"It is bedtime, I know," she began. "We should choose something quiet, but it is so fun to play happy music with you. Let's be playful!"

The king laughed aloud at her request. "Playful it shall be!" He gathered up his harp and began plucking gaily at the strings. Abishag listened for a moment until she could harmonize into the music. The king's fingers moved magically, but his eyes were fixed on Abishag's face, as if monitoring the pleasure he was providing.

Seeing him watch her, Abishag self-consciously dropped her gaze to the floor. Still, her fingers kept pace with the king's music. The notes they played danced together through the darkening room.

"Could you do this all night?" the king asked above the music.

"Only with you," Abishag replied.

CHAPTER 25

THE MORNING SUN PEEKED THROUGH a gap in the heavy curtains. Abishag stretched lazily and settled back down into the warmth of her tumbled bed like a kitten changing positions. She listened for the king's breaths across the room. They were still the slow, even breaths of sleep. How entrenched into her heart was the well being of this man, so that even the sound of his breathing comforted her.

Abishag curled deeper into her nest of blankets and relived the memory of the night before. A smile washed across her lips as she recalled the music they had played together. Behind her closed eyes, she could see the happiness on the king's face, and she could almost hear the harps' song. It had been a juncture in the paths of their two lives that bound them together. In her heart anyway.

No doubt the king would discount the value of their moments together; but he had thought to do it for her, and that alone endeared him to her. Her memories of moments with the king would become a bouquet of countless small ecstasies, though an insignificant collection of miscellaneous moments to anyone else. She had few enough things to call her own. Delightful memories were cherished possessions.

Abishag's thoughts returned to the queen's conversation with the king from the previous night. It was true. Solomon was of marrying age. Rachel's suggestion that Abishag might be given to young Solomon festered in her mind. Though she enjoyed Solomon's company in a group, there was no tug at her heart when she thought of him. *Why not?* she wondered. He had treated her kindly since they first met. He was near Joseph's age, and he was, oh, so handsome! She had witnessed other eligible young women vie for his attention.

Still, Solomon simply did not flutter her pulse. To be honest, Joseph had not either. She never felt more alive than in the presence of the king. The friendship she had formed with him dulled her appetite for any other relationship. She feared that no other man would ever seem to her as wise, as gentle, or as affectionate as King David.

How odd that young, virile Solomon cannot spark an interest in me, she thought. Perhaps it did not happen because Abishag had never reconciled herself to the permanence of giving Jezreel her place beside Joseph? A family with Joseph had been the only dream she had known as a young woman. Perhaps Abishag felt socially inferior to the beautiful women who were being considered as a mate for the next king. Perhaps Solomon's confident exuberance intimidated her. *Perhaps my heart is reluctant to embrace another man who might be taken from me.*

It was ridiculous to imagine becoming Solomon's wife! On the other hand, having seen the glint in the young prince's eyes when in the company of beautiful women, it was not difficult to imagine the collection of concubines he might put together. Might Rachel be correct about Abishag's fate? She shook her head violently. *I will be no man's concubine!*

Had her friend Rachel also once scorned her eventual destiny? Was she a woman who could offer her heart's love to a man and then be content to be needed, however briefly, for only occasional pleasures in bed? Rachel's love for the king hovered just above the surface of every breath she took. There was no mistaking it. It had outlasted her usefulness to the king. Still, Rachel seemed to show none of the bitterness that consumed the other women in the concubines' quarters. What was her secret?

As if on cue, the chamber doors opened. Rachel stepped quietly into the entry, her arms hugging the fresh robe and linens for the morning bath. Abishag sat upright in bed and waved gaily to her friend.

Rachel unloaded her arms and then slipped into the partitioned area. "How lazy you are being today," she whispered with a smile.

"It is late, isn't it?" Abishag agreed. "It seemed unnecessary to stir about and wake the king when he is sleeping so soundly."

"You were up quite late," Rachel commented. Abishag offered a surprised look. "The music could be heard in the great hallway. I stood in the shadows and listened until you stopped."

"Oh! It did not occur to me that we might be keeping others awake."

"Music of the harp is never disturbing. How I envy your ability to play."

"My abilities with the harp are meager compared to the king's," Abishag said. "Alone, my music would not have caught your ear. It was the blended harmony of the two instruments that made the music sweet."

And it was the company of the king that you truly envied, Abishag thought sadly. She stared into the eyes of this woman who so carefully guarded her affection for the king. Abishag envied her ability. But this morning, there was a weariness in Rachel's face she had not seen before.

"Sit down for a few minutes." Abishag patted a spot next to her on the bed. Rachel sat down carefully. "I think the music kept you awake too late into the night. You look tired."

Rachel smiled self-consciously. "I am not as young as you."

"Why did you stay in the hallway so late?"

"Because the music was beautiful, and I knew how pleased the king was to be playing. He has not enjoyed that pleasure for a long time." Genuine happiness for the king danced in her words.

"Did he ever play for you?" Abishag asked.

"Oh, yes!" Then Rachel's smile faded as she added, "He played for all of us." Her voice suggested that the king's music had lasted only as long as his interest in each of the concubines. "But none of us were ever able to play with him. You are special in that way."

Abishag's heart leapt at this distinction from the king's concubines. For once, it had nothing to do with her appearance or nursing abilities. She was special because she could pluck the strings of a harp to please her king. The concubines had pleasured only the king's body, and only until he could no longer respond to them; but the music would pleasure the king's heart as long as he lived. There might be other joys she would never share with him, but the passion of music was uniquely theirs to enjoy. Rachel had a way of gently pointing out advantages Abishag overlooked. *What a dear friend she has become!*

"Tonight you must get some extra rest," she encouraged Rachel. "I have never seen you looking so weary. Has it become too taxing to keep the king's chambers supplied?"

"No. It gives me excuse to escape from the bickering sourness of the other women."

"Have you ever considered asking for separate accommodations?" Abishag asked.

"Certainly not. I suppose I have the option of living with my children, but they do not need an old woman to care for."

Abishag's lips puckered into a disapproving smile. "You are not an 'old woman,' Rachel. You are a beautiful woman with a heart as generous as any I have ever known. It seems impossible that there are no men anywhere in this city who would want to marry one such as you."

"Marry me? Ha!" Rachel scoffed. "Men want young lovers for wives to breed for heirs. They can pay for the maid services I might provide. No need to saddle themselves with the likes of me."

"Are all men so short-sighted?" Abishag reached over and squeezed her friend's hand. Immediately she pulled her hand away. Rachel's skin was fiery hot. "You are ill! How long have you had this fever?"

"A couple of days," Rachel admitted.

"You should be in bed." Abishag stood and went to wet a cloth to cool Rachel's face. "Lie down on my bed." Rachel had no strength to object.

Abishag straightened the blankets and folded them at the foot of the bed. The cool cloth might cause chills. If so, the blankets would be ready. Rachel quickly drifted off to a restless sleep, as if she had been waiting for permission. When her bare arms began to quiver with chills, Abishag pulled the blankets up and tucked them close to her body. Before long, Rachel tossed the blankets aside. Her face glistened with fever.

Abishag stood anxiously at the end of the partitions so that she could see both Rachel and the king. He would waken soon, and she would need to leave Rachel's bedside to tend to him. Perhaps when he heard how ill Rachel was, he would ask Bathsheba to remove her from the concubines' quarters. No doubt he would assign Abishag to care for her. Any new lodging for Rachel would become Abishag's as well.

Rachel immediately drifted off again, her breathing labored by the congestion from lying down. She unconsciously reached for blankets. Abishag pulled them up for her and tucked them close. She slipped over to the fireplace and hung some of the king's blankets over the steam to warm. He had not needed the steamed blankets for some time now.

"Good morning, Abishag." The king's greeting startled her.

"Good morning, my lord," she responded over her shoulder as she hung the blankets.

"Are you anticipating cold weather?"

Abishag did not answer until she was at his bedside. "No, my lord. Rachel is very ill. In fact, she is lying on my bed just now. The blankets are for her." She waited anxiously for the king to grant his consent.

"She is here? Why?" he king asked.

"She brought fresh linens for today, but she looked so exhausted that I invited her to sit for a few minutes. Then I realized she was burning up with a fever. I could not send her back to her quarters. She needs quiet rest."

"You intend to nurse her here?" His question lacked the compassion Abishag had hoped Rachel's condition would elicit.

"Only until other accommodations can be made." Abishag struggled to choose her words.

"What other accommodations do you suggest?"

Abishag swallowed hard. "Surely in so large a palace, an empty room could be found and set up for her."

"I hardly think the concubines' accommodations lack for comfort," he responded.

"You cannot begin to imagine the constant bickering that goes on there," Abishag said. "It would be impossible for Rachel to rest there."

"I suppose that means you will be staying with her to care for her?" For a moment, Abishag imagined a shadow of disappointment in the king's words.

"She will not need constant attention," Abishag assured him.

"Very well. When the queen visits this morning, we will ask her to find a room for Rachel."

"Thank you, my lord," Abishag whispered. "Rachel will be most grateful."

"Tend to her carefully. It is clear that she has been a good friend for you." At last, Abishag detected a glimmer of affection in his words, redeeming him from Abishag's silent disapproval.

"Yes, she has been a very good friend. She is also the mother of three of your children," she reminded him gently.

"I have not forgotten," the king said.

How long had it been since he had seen those children? The question teetered on the tip of her tongue, but in the end she did not ask. Further, was he aware of what had become of the children since they had grown up? Had he comforted Rachel when Shiloh died?

"I know you do not understand the relationship between a king and his concubines," the king said. "No amount of explaining would make it clear to someone who is so ruled by her heart as you are. I can only assure you that I have cared for the women and children involved as carefully as tradition allows."

"Then please do not question my request that Rachel be moved out of the concubines' quarters." Abishag could not bear to harbor disapproval for the king.

"Bathsheba will make the arrangements," the king answered with a tone of finality to his words.

Abishag nodded and lowered her eyes. "I will get your breakfast." Perhaps she had been too bold to request the move for Rachel, but her allegiance to the friendship had demanded that she speak. She carried the breakfast tray to the king's bedside table and removed the lids from his meal. She carefully positioned the tray over the king's lap then turned away from him.

"Have you eaten?" he asked as she retreated.

"I will share my breakfast with Rachel when she wakens," Abishag answered over her shoulder.

"Nonsense!" the king retorted. "More food can be brought for her, or delivered to her room when she is settled." He struggled to keep his impatience in check. "Please bring your tray and join me. I have grown accustomed to enjoying breakfast with you."

"It is so late now that the queen will arrive shortly, and she will provide company for you." Abishag's heart grasped at the affection she sensed in the king's invitation, but it was difficult to reconcile the affection he showed her with his seeming apathy toward a woman who had borne him children.

"As you wish," he responded. "When you are not so disappointed with me, perhaps you will agree to keep me company again."

Abishag bristled at his suggestion that she had taken offense without cause and that he would wait for her tantrum to calm. Still, it seemed inappropriate for her to find fault with the king. She swallowed her reply and disappeared behind her partitions.

Rachel began to stir, but she was still feverish enough that Abishag doubted she had overheard her conversation with the king. She dipped the cloth in the cool water and wiped Rachel's forehead. Eyes glazed with pain fluttered then closed again.

Abishag heard the chamber doors open and knew the queen had come for her morning visit. She was counting on Bathsheba's kindness to provide a room for Rachael. She listened carefully to hear how the king would phrase the request.

"Your breakfast is rather late," the queen observed as she approached the king's bed. "Where is Abishag?"

"Good morning, Bathsheba," the king greeted, ignoring her questions for the moment. "Come, sit down with me. You have been assigned the task of keeping me company while I eat my breakfast. You are just in time."

"Why are you just now eating?"

"Abishag allowed me to be lazy this morning," the king answered. "She is busy caring for another patient."

"Who is ill?" Bathsheba asked.

"It is Rachel. Abishag is concerned. She would like a private room prepared for Rachel."

Abishag's heart froze waiting for the queen's response.

"A private room? Is that really necessary?"

"Abishag believes it is, my dear." The king spoke in a whisper. "Surely there is some room she could use."

"Of course, but I wonder if you make this request as much for Rachel's welfare as for your dread of denying Abishag anything."

"Perhaps it is both," the king conceded with a quiet laugh. "It need not be a permanent arrangement—just until Rachel recovers."

"I will take care of it," the queen promised. "Now, tell me why you were so lazy this morning."

The king clanked his silverware against the dish. "We were up late last night," he offered. "We played our harps together, and the hour grew late before we knew it."

"You are playing your harp again?" Bathsheba asked incredulously.

"Yes. It seems to be something this old man cannot forget how to do."

"I would not have expected you to forget how to play your harp," the queen replied, "but I was not certain the stiffness in your fingers would allow it. It must have been encouraging to rediscover the pleasure you always found in your music."

"My fingers are stiff, to be sure, but the delightful music seems to loosen them." The king finished his breakfast and settled back into the pillows with a sigh. "I slept soundly afterwards. It seems the playing was a wonderful tranquilizer for me. We agreed that we must do it again soon."

"It pleases me that you enjoyed yourself so thoroughly," Bathsheba said. "What makes you happy makes me happy."

The king reached for Bathsheba's hand and patted it. "So it has always been with you. That is perhaps the difference that has most endeared you to me."

"There is nothing to be gained in begrudging your happiness. On the contrary, I have found that my days are more pleasant when you are smiling." They laughed together. Then a comfortable silence settled between them.

After a few minutes, Bathsheba stood and gathered the breakfast dishes onto the tray. "I will go now and see what arrangements can be made for Rachel. If Abishag is nursing her for a few days, perhaps it is time to see if Adonijah can manage without her visits."

Abishag caught her breath at the queen's suggestion. She was not consciously listening to the conversation beyond her partitions, but her ears were alerted at the mention of Adonijah's name.

"Today I will make a trip to his chambers and see how he fares," the king announced. "It may be that he has grown fond of having Abishag around and will not be anxious to dismiss her. I have seen sparks of interest in his eyes when she is present." The king had lowered his voice, but Abishag's dread of Adonijah forced her ears to strain, and she did not miss the king's suggestion of attraction between his son and his nurse. Her stomach knotted at the thought.

"It would be good for you to visit," the queen agreed. "You should remember that Abishag is in the palace for *your* welfare, and not his. She will be distracted from your care enough with worrying about Rachel." She paused to offer room for the king's objection, but none was given. "I will send word to Abishag as soon as a room is prepared." Her gowns rustled slightly as she left the room.

CHAPTER 26

JUST AS SHE PROMISED, THE queen prepared a room for Rachel and sent a servant to inform Abishag and the king. Abishag bundled her friend in a freshly steamed blanket and supported her through the corridor. Rachel's new accommodations were small but adequate for the purpose of quiet rest. Abishag settled Rachel into the softness of the bed and she soon fell into a restless sleep.

For a few minutes, Abishag sat next to the bed and watched the labored breathing of her friend. The vigil reminded her of caring for her mother, and it struck her that Rachel's children should be notified of their mother's illness. In all probability, Rachel would recover completely, but her children should still be alerted. Abishag had no idea how to contact either of them. No doubt, the king had as little knowledge of his children's whereabouts as Abishag. It would be necessary to approach the queen for help in this situation.

Convinced that Rachel was sleeping as comfortably as possible, Abishag slipped out of the room and returned to the king's chambers. The morning had been consumed with caring for Rachel's needs, and the morning tasks she usually performed for the king had gone undone. Still, if she wasted no time, she could catch up on the most important chores. It would not be good to give the queen reason to think Rachel was being cared for at the expense of the king. There would be time to help him bathe before his noon meal was served. She gathered the bathing supplies that Rachel had delivered earlier.

Turning toward the king, Abishag found him sitting in his chair, watching her hurried steps. "There is no need to rush about so. I am not an impatient man." When Abishag paused long enough to meet his eyes, he asked, "Are Rachel's new accommodations acceptable?"

"The queen has provided a secluded room where Rachel can rest undisturbed. I appreciate your assistance with the arrangements," Abishag answered. Though there were thanks to be given the queen, it was true that the king had spared Abishag the unpleasantness of requesting the queen's understanding herself.

"You are welcome, child. Hopefully, you will forgive my youthful indiscretions and see that I am not completely unfeeling in matters that involve the women of my household." He paused until Abishag looked into his eyes and a conciliatory smile was offered.

Abishag found his smile irresistible and warmly returned it. How much better it felt to be agreeable with the king than to harbor resentment for the insensitivity she had privately accused him of displaying. It would be easier now with a forgiving heart to review the ecstasies of the previous night. And she did intend to review those ecstasies! She began the king's bath.

"I would like to visit Adonijah today," he said. "Would you be able to accompany me?"

Abishag instinctively pulled back her hand, as if to protect herself from the mere mention of Adonijah's name.

The king looked at her quizzically.

She hurried her answer to avoid being questioned. "I will accompany you wherever you wish to go, my lord."

"You have become a delightful companion, child," the king declared. "It is settled. We will visit Adonijah after our meal. You must be starved. I hardly think you took the time this morning for your breakfast."

"I was not hungry until you mentioned it," Abishag replied with a smile. "Now, you'd best guard your portion or I might help myself."

"I will gladly share. I am seldom hungry. Old age takes care of a lot of appetites. Mostly, I finish my meals just to please you and to avoid Bathsheba's scowl."

"Is there nothing that can tickle your palate?" Abishag asked.

"Enjoying your company and seeing that you are well fed is enough satisfaction for me." He reached for Abishag's hand and stopped the bathing.

"You keep my belly quite content," Abishag assured him. "But I wish you would think of something that I could get for you as an occasional treat."

The king laughed aloud at her request. "Why is it so important that you treat me?"

Abishag finished his bath and organized the supplies on the tray. "You, my lord, are in the position of being the giver so much of the time. Do you not enjoy it? Is it so difficult to imagine the pleasure I might get from giving to you?"

Noting the logic of her request, the king responded, "It is, indeed, a pleasure to give, especially to someone who is so easily pleased; but I have need of nothing, and my age has eliminated most of the desires I once thought so necessary."

Abishag's lips pulled to one side in unappeased resignation. She picked up the bathing tray and turned to put them away. Before she was out of reach, the king gently took hold of her elbow.

"There is one thing you have given me from the very beginning, Abishag. One thing that I both want and need the rest of my life— pleasant companionship." The king spoke softly and looked directly into her eyes. "It does not matter that your gift to me has not cost you anything. I cherish your friendship more than anything your money could buy."

"I had hoped you would think of something that I alone could give you. You have many friends. I have become your companion by assignment. It is not as if you choose to have me around each day." Abishag's words boldly gave voice to her feelings, almost against her will. Hearing them spoken seemed to display nothing but selfishness, and she regretted her honesty.

"No two friends are alike, child," the king responded. "No one person can fulfill all the needs of another person." He paused, as if considering how much of his soul to reveal to the girl. "And, by the way, I do choose to have you around each day."

"You dare not defy the queen's wishes to have me here," Abishag countered with a faint smile.

"I have no desire to defy the queen's wishes to have you here. I enjoy you. You have rubbed new life into my bones. A new friendship like ours is a bonus for such an old man." He laughed aloud, and the sobriety in the air vanished.

While they ate, Abishag listened to the king's review of the celebration events she had not attended. He told her about the unknown contestant who had outdistanced all the other runners in the foot races. The man from a small village had been secretly running for miles in the dark each evening, after his family had gone to bed. No one expected him to participate in the races, let alone win so easily. The king then described the heated ruckus that developed after the wrestling competition. He lathered over the savory feasts the queen had arranged.

"If you want to hear about the women's lavish gowns at the closing gala, you will need to ask the queen for a report," the king finished. "I dare say the money represented by the new gowns at the gala could have funded this kingdom for a decade." He stacked the empty dishes and placed the cover over them. "Perhaps you would like to check on Rachel before we take our walk to see Adonijah? I have kept you occupied too long this morning."

Abishag stood and lifted the tray. "Yes, my lord, I would like to see if she has wakened. I will not be gone long. You can rest up for the visit while I am out."

"There is no hurry," the king said. "Please stay with Rachel for as long as you are needed."

CHAPTER 27

RACHEL WAKENED, BUT HER FEVER had not subsided. Abishag carried a bowl of fresh water to the bedside and wiped her friend's face. Her dark hair twisted into unruly curls from perspiration. Abishag pushed the damp curls back from Rachel's white face. Heavy circles under her eyes darkened against the pallor of her cheeks. How had Abishag missed these symptoms?

She stoked the fireplace and erected a makeshift line for steaming blankets. Then she set the pot of water closer to the fire and waited impatiently for the steam to moisten the air in the room. Out of the herb box, she selected ingredients to add to the water to fill the room with soothing aromas. Other herbs she crushed into powder and poured into Rachel's cup. All the while, she struggled not to remember how her mother had slipped away from her with a similar fever.

Abishag lifted her friend's head and coaxed her to sip the medicated water. Unwilling lips tightened against the intruding cup. The herbs lent a brackish taste to the water.

"Please, Rachel," Abishag begged, "you need to drink this. It will help break the fever, and you will be able to rest."

"Who are you?" Rachel demanded in a whisper. "You will poison me!"

"It is I, Abishag." The fever was making Rachel delirious, but she had no strength to fight her imagined enemy. "I am your friend. I will not poison you."

"Let me die," Rachel implored.

"You are too young to die," Abishag argued. "I need you. Please drink." She pried Rachel's lips apart and tipped the cup. If she swallowed enough of the mixture, the herbs would soon relax her and she would fall into a drugged sleep. Abishag tucked the blankets close around her friend, but Rachel thrashed against them until she had bared her arms and legs.

Finally the flailing stopped, and Rachel's breaths slowed to a steady pace. Her eyes fluttered a few more times, then sleep overtook her. Abishag gathered a steamed blanket to replace the blanket that had been tossed aside. Satisfied that Rachel would rest for a while, she tiptoed out the door and hurried back to the king's chambers.

"If Rachel needs you, we can visit Adonijah another time," the king offered.

"She is resting now," Abishag responded. "No need to change our plans." Indeed, she was anxious for the king to see his son. It would be impossible for him not to see that Adonijah could resume his own care. She would be released from the grip he had held her with for so many days.

Abishag bent to slip the king's slippers over his feet. Standing, she braced her legs to assist him out of his chair. She stepped in front of him to prevent him from moving until his balance was sure. Satisfied, she moved to his side and slipped her arm behind his elbow. There was a comfort she enjoyed standing so close to the king. She would savor the few minutes it would take to walk down the corridor to Adonijah's quarters.

"You are quiet," the king observed as they neared the chamber doors. He reached up and patted her hand. "Rachel has not improved, has she?"

"No," Abishag admitted. "I cannot know for sure how long the fever afflicted her before I noticed, but it is not good that it still persists. It is time to notify her children." Rachel's children—the king's children. It seemed impossible that they could be both.

"I will dispatch a courier to bring Joshua in from his post. He will know how to get word to his sister."

"Thank you," Abishag said. "I hope they will be able to come immediately."

"You are very worried about Rachel, aren't you?" The king stopped in the middle of the corridor to observe how Abishag would answer.

"I only know that few in Shunem have survived such a high fever." She tugged gently on the king's arm. The sooner the unpleasant task of visiting Adonijah was over, the sooner she could return to Rachel's bedside.

Elan excused himself when he saw that Adonijah's father had come to visit. Abishag watched with disgust as he retreated out of sight.

"Father, how good to see you!" Adonijah sat propped with pillows in his bed, though for no physical reason that Abishag could see. She was more familiar with his body than she wanted to be, and she was certain that his worst injuries had healed. He should easily be up and about by this time. Perhaps she and the king had interrupted something between Adonijah and Elan.

"Abishag has reported to me how well you have recovered," the king said. "Still, you are in bed so late in the day."

"It may be that Abishag is rushing tales of my recovery to defend her stunning reputation as a nursemaid," Adonijah suggested.

"There would be no need for her to defend her reputation to me," the king said. "I am proof enough of her nursing capabilities. She has voiced concern that you have not been up and exercising enough to prevent your muscles from stiffening."

"Indeed? I wonder, if she had sustained such injuries, would she be so anxious to jump to her feet?" Adonijah's eyes sparked with fury.

"No need to be defensive, Adonijah. Abishag's admonition to keep your muscles moving is sound advice. Speaking from experience, the pain of immediate movement is considerably less than the pain of delayed movement."

Adonijah was clearly perturbed with the report Abishag had given the king. "This is hardly my first injury, Father, nor will it be my last. I am well aware of the threat of stiffness, and I have been exercising more than your maid knows." He cast a snarling glare toward Abishag.

"Excellent!" the king said. "It seems, then, that you will no longer need the daily services of Abishag. What fortunate timing since she has another patient for whom she must care."

"You, Father?" Adonijah guessed. "Is it you who needs the daily services of this girl? Here you are standing before me, on your own and in improved health, but still she sleeps in your chambers?" He paused dramatically. "By all means, release her from the responsibility of tending my wounds so that she may devote her full attention to you again."

Abishag watched the fiery exchange from a distance. There was no mistaking the king's displeasure with Adonijah's insinuations, but he offered no reprimand. Had Adonijah been a soldier in the king's army and spoken to the king with such a tone, she dared not think what his fate might have been.

"You incorrectly assume that I have begrudged Abishag's time with you, my son. It is not I who needs her most just now, but one of the women of the court." The king's voice was strangely mellow.

"At any rate, I am pleased to see that you are doing so well. I look forward to the resumption of your visits to my chambers."

A sigh of relief escaped Abishag's lips as they left Adonijah's quarters. She would no longer be expected to care for Adonijah. Had water been available, she would have scrubbed the touch of him from her fingers. Indeed, had privacy been available as well, she would have immersed her entire body and scrubbed savagely to eradicate any trace of Adonijah's handprints.

Elan waited impatiently outside the chamber doors. He bowed deeply as the king passed, but he cast a vengeful look at Abishag. *How delighted he will be,* she mused, *to find out that I will no longer be visiting his friend.* She held her head high with disregard, but she knew she could not ignore the threat that Elan might still mean her harm. And he would have Adonijah's blessing.

No, I must still be wary of that man's hatred. She slipped her arm into the king's, comforted by his closeness.

CHAPTER 28

A COURIER HAD BEEN SENT TO notify Joshua of his mother's illness, and he appeared in Rachel's doorway within hours. He found Abishag leaned over his mother's bedside, gently wiping her face and fussing over her blankets.

"Excuse me," he whispered.

His voice startled Abishag, and she turned quickly to see who had spoken. There was no mistaking that this was Rachel's son Joshua. He had the well-exercised physique of a soldier and sun-browned skin. Short, dark curls framed his face. A handsome face, it was.

"You must be Joshua," Abishag stammered.

"I am. I did not mean to frighten you."

"I was not expecting you to come so quickly," Abishag said. "Please, come closer to your mother's bed. She is sleeping now, but it will be good for her to see your face when she wakens."

Joshua hurried to his mother's side. His fearful look seemed out of place on a soldier's face, but Abishag was not free to dismiss it. "The courier reported that Mother's condition is serious. Has she improved any?" He reached to hold Rachel's hand, then hesitated lest he disturb her sleep.

"The fever persists, I'm afraid," Abishag whispered. "Your mother is a strong woman, Joshua, and she ignored her illness too long."

"Has Hannah arrived yet?"

"No. I am not aware of how far she had to travel. We had to rely upon your contacting her. Rachel never told me where Hannah lives, and she was too ill to ask in this condition."

"The officer's house is not far from the palace. She should be here soon." Joshua seemed anxious for his sister's presence to lighten the burden of his fears for his mother's sake.

"Your mother has talked often about you," Abishag offered. "She is proud of her children."

"She has always been a good mother," Joshua responded. "It could not have been easy for her, raising us alone as she did."

Abishag tried to imagine childhood without her father. It seemed impossible that a child could mature without the love and protection a father provides, but the man who stood before her wore the confidence of a content adult.

"Tell me your name," Joshua said. "Mother has written to me about her new friend at the palace who had been appointed to care for the king. Is it you?"

"I am Abishag. Your mother rescued me from a lonely existence in an unfamiliar place. She has a kind heart. I have been fortunate to become acquainted with her."

"Her letters described you perfectly," Joshua said. "It was difficult to believe that there could be a woman so beautiful and yet so common as Mother claimed you to be."

"I can't imagine why Rachel would mention me in her letters, but she was generous in her assessment of my looks and correct in her placement of me among the common people. Moving into the palace was like moving to a foreign land. She explained much about life in the palace, and more than once she prevented my bungling proper behavior among royalty."

Though they whispered, their conversation woke Rachel. Abishag prayed that the earlier delirium had passed and that Rachel would recognize and welcome her son. Rachel pulled her arms free of the blankets and turned to see whose voices she heard.

"Joshua! Is that really you?" Her words were slow and labored, but clearly she was aware of her son's company.

"Yes, Mother," Joshua answered tenderly. He stepped closer to her bedside and knelt to kiss her feverish hand.

"If you have been summoned, I must be gravely ill," Rachel said with a weak smile. "Is Hannah here as well?"

"She is on her way. We are grateful that Abishag notified us. We would have wanted to know. Are you feeling any better?"

Rachel closed her eyes and sighed heavily. "I am very tired, and all I have done is sleep."

"You were too stubborn to get the rest you needed earlier," Joshua chided her lovingly. "So now you have no choice."

"No sympathy from you," his mother whispered. She squeezed Joshua's hand, expressing the love her words were too faint to utter. "You have met Abishag. Is she not everything I said?" She spoke with her eyes closed. Abishag felt her face flush at the realization that Rachel had been promoting her to Joshua.

"We have only just met, Mother, but I easily identified her as the one you had described." Joshua allowed a quick look at Abishag. "I had thought perhaps you had exaggerated her attributes, but I see that you did not."

Abishag busied herself preparing more herbs. She was not certain how she felt about Rachel's plan. Joshua was only five years older than she, and he was not married. Still, she remembered how Rachel had explained that he avoided opportunities for relationships with young women. Love, as he had witnessed it in his mother's life, had not brought the happiness she deserved. His older sister had settled for even less and had sold her body to the highest bidders. It seemed unwise for him to allow his heart to consider any woman.

Joshua conversed easily with his mother. Abishag was not uncomfortable in his presence, but she could not say there was any immediate attraction to him. The truth was, her heart was not available to Joshua, or to any other man except the king. How ridiculous that would sound if she admitted it to anyone. Rachel was aware of her feelings for the king. Indeed, they were not so unlike her own feelings for the man. Why then had she thought to match Abishag with her only son?

A quiet knock at the door ended all thought of the king. Abishag opened the door and met a frightened young woman. *This must be Hannah*, Abishag thought to herself. Rachel's family was complete now . . . except for the presence of the king.

"I am Hannah, Rachel's daughter," the girl explained.

"Come in," Abishag urged. "Joshua is here with your mother. He told her you would be coming. She will be glad to see you."

"I was told she is seriously ill. Has there been any improvement?" Hannah's eyes begged for news that the fever had broken and the threat to her mother's life was over. Abishag could not offer that comfort.

"Go to her," she said simply.

Joshua moved aside and made room for his sister to greet their mother. With the total abandon of a loving friendship, Hannah leaned over the motionless form of her mother and kissed her pale cheek. "I am here, Mother."

"Hannah! You are both here now. I want nothing more." Rachel spoke with forced effort.

"What can I do for you, Mother?" Hannah asked tenderly.

"There is nothing for anyone to do," Rachel replied. "Just be here with me."

"I will go nowhere," her daughter promised. "I will be here to help you out of bed, and soon we will walk together in the gardens."

Rachel turned her head to face her daughter. "It is enough that you are here."

Abishag had the medicine prepared and thought it best to administer it without delay. "Rachel, I have another drink for you. Would you like Hannah to help you this time?"

"You waste your herbs, Abishag," was her soft reply.

"Mother, do not say that," Hannah rebuked. "Let me help you. Easy now." She lifted her mother's head and cradled it gently with one arm. Abishag handed the cup to her, and Hannah tipped it slowly. Rachel swallowed the liquid, wincing at the taste. "We will let you rest now," Hannah said.

With her children at her side, Rachel died quietly in the night. Her passing was insignificant news in the palace; but to the three who had kept vigil at her bedside, the loss was staggering. Even after Rachel's last breath was silenced, they stood beside her, unwilling to sever their hearts from hers.

Abishag's grief multiplied as she watched Rachel's children grasp the finality of their last few moments with their mother. Hannah clung to Rachel's lifeless hand. Her tears flowed freely. Joshua stood stoically behind his sister, with a gentle arm around her shoulders. Tears welled up behind the soldier's determination to appear untouched, but occasionally he raised his free hand and wiped across his eyes.

One by one, God was snuffing the important people out of Abishag's life. The numbing pain of losing Rachel festered into silent anger. Would God leave her no one to wrap her heart around? The palace suddenly loomed over her like the unwelcoming beast it had seemed only months ago when she had stepped inside its boundaries for the first time.

Abishag dared not speak and shatter the tender farewell she was witnessing. How fortunate that Rachel's children had been called when they were. They had little enough time with their mother as it was. Now, the service would need to be planned, and the exhausting business of that ordeal would numb their minds for a while.

Joshua turned and stepped toward her. He held out one hand and gently wrapped his fingers around Abishag's small hand. "You were a good friend to my mother. Thank you."

"Her life here in the palace was not easy," Abishag whispered. "You and Hannah gave her reason to carry on. Everything she did was for her children." Abishag watched the chiseled features of Joshua's face as he struggled to control his emotions.

"I should have moved her out of this place," Joshua said through gritted teeth. "She deserved a home of her own, but she would not hear of it; and finally I did not mention it anymore." His eyes met Abishag's. She could see the anger that he tried to veil. "What good did it do for her to stay here?"

Abishag touched his arm. "It is not easy to explain a woman's heart, Joshua. Your mother loved your father very much. It seemed to comfort her to be close to him."

"How could she love someone who had forgotten she even existed?"

"For some people, opening their heart to another person is a lifetime commitment. Their love for that person expands to fill every part of their being, and there is no desire for anyone else. Even if that love is not returned." Abishag lowered her head to escape the piercing intensity of Joshua's eyes.

"You have loved like that, haven't you?" Joshua asked softly.

"I have," Abishag admitted without looking at him.

"Isn't that a waste of many years for one as young as you?"

"Your mother was no older than I am when she met the king," Abishag said.

"It was most certainly a waste of many of my mother's years. Can't you see that it would be the same for you?" Joshua's voice was tender.

"How is loving someone a waste?" Abishag questioned. "Have you never loved a woman? Have you never felt the fire of an all-consuming passion? So that every fiber of your being rejoices in the presence of the one you love—and aches in separation from her? So that the very thought of her makes you smile? So that her welfare and happiness become more important than your own? When you have loved like that, you will understand that your mother's love was not wasted." Abishag's heart beat wildly as she defended both Rachel's and her own feelings for the king.

"If that love is not returned, what is there to sustain it? Isn't there an overpowering sense of rejection?" It was obvious that Joshua had struggled in the past with his mother's devotion to the king.

"That is difficult to answer," Abishag said. "For your mother, I think that caring for her children was enough. There comes a resignation to unrequited love. In the end, it is enough to know that you have loved someone so deeply." She paused again. "How can you be so certain that your mother's love was not returned?"

Joshua looked at her in disbelief. "How can there be any question? My mother was only one of many women the king used for his own entertainment. He did not make her his wife. He did not even ask for her company after a few years. You tell me. Did he love her?"

"Don't be too quick to condemn your father, Joshua. Just as there are some who love with undivided affection, there are some who seem capable of sharing great love with more than one person. Who is to say which is better?"

CHAPTER 29

JOSHUA RETURNED TO HIS POST a week after his mother's burial. Abishag often reviewed that last conversation she had with him. She knew Rachel would never have admitted that her life had been wasted. Still, she had warned Abishag of the danger in giving her heart to the king. Too late, it seemed.

Life for Abishag returned to the routine of caring for the king. When the weather warmed, he asked almost daily to walk in the gardens. Abishag looked forward to those times. While they walked, it was easier to imagine the king to be vibrantly healthy and free from the threat of dying than it was while caring for him in his bed. He named the flowers as they strolled, and his fingers occasionally reached to touch their beauty. The sun restored color to his face and brightened the sparkle in his eyes. At times, they talked with ease; sometimes they walked in silence. Always, the walks left him exhausted.

It was this that worried Abishag more than anything. The recovery of his strength seemed to have reached a plateau. Now, it was declining again. He began asking to prepare for bed earlier and earlier. He slept fitfully. He ate more to satisfy Abishag than to satisfy his own appetite. Though he seemed willing to listen to her chatter, he had little to add. Their harps sat idle.

"Remember how you once warmed my blankets over the fire?" he asked one night. His question startled Abishag. The evenings were still warm. She seldom used a blanket.

"I remember."

"Could you do that again?" He seemed hesitant to ask it of her, knowing she would assume the worst.

"If it makes you more comfortable, I will warm them at once." She stepped out the door and requested more wood for the fire. "For now, let me add a heavier blanket." She tucked the blanket close to the king's legs. His eyes closed wearily, and his breaths came slow and deep.

Occasionally, he opened his eyes to watch her. "I am a rickety old man," he said with a tired smile. "Life is not much fun anymore."

Abishag's heart froze. She was not prepared for this conversation. "What can I do to make it fun again?"

The king frowned in disapproval. "It is not your responsibility to make my life fun, child. It is the cycle of life. One dies and another is born."

"There will never be another one to replace you," Abishag argued.

The king reached for her hand. "There are some who would cheer that fact." He squeezed her hand and rubbed his thumb back and forth on her palm. As intended, his touch soothed Abishag's frightened heart. There seemed nothing more she could say. The fire dimmed to red coals before the king's hand slipped away from hers in sleep.

Solomon visited more often now. In the summer months, the sheep flocks were pastured high in the hills where it was cooler.

Although the king had regularly sent Solomon to assess his flocks, lately Solomon stayed close to home. His visits cheered the king.

Abishag excused herself when Solomon came, but she never ventured outside the king's chambers. The king's conversations with his son were not meant to be private. There was no missing the truth that Solomon was being given last-minute training from his dying father. They talked about the men with leadership responsibilities. Once in a while, the king gave advice on how to find a way to remove one of the men from office. Suggestions for replacements were given and discussed at length.

The liveliest conversation always involved the temple. There were scrolls with plans for the building, and the two men talked at length about its construction. Material had been collected for several years already. Though he never mentioned it to Abishag, she thought she heard regret in the king's voice when he reminded Solomon that it would be a great privilege for him to build the temple for his God. As important as the temple seemed to the king, Abishag wondered why he had not built it himself. One day, she asked.

The king considered his answer carefully. "Our God is gracious to forgive our sins, but He has not promised to remove the consequences. There is no sin without consequence. Where would be the lesson if the penalties could be so easily disregarded?" He sighed and turned to look at Abishag. A gentle smile framed his wise face.

"I have sinned against my God many times. He has forgiven me each time, but one consequence was that I would not be permitted to build the temple. Still, God promised that my son Solomon would construct it, and I am thankful for that."

"It has been a project you have enjoyed together," Abishag said. "In some ways, you have helped build it."

"In some ways, I have," he agreed. "One day when you have children of your own you will understand how precious it is to see them succeed. With this weary body, watching Solomon's enthusiasm for planning the temple is as much pleasure as I can handle. But it is a genuine pleasure. Another gift from God."

The king held out his hand to invite Abishag to step closer. She put her hand in his and felt his fingers wrap around hers. How could such a simple act bring her such peace? It was as if merely touching the king connected her to his source of comfort. She swallowed hard, willing her tears to dissolve.

With her hand tucked warmly in his, the king pulled her closer to his bed. Abishag sensed that he was struggling to put his thoughts into words, and she was certain they were thoughts that would be difficult for her to hear. The afternoon shadows darkened the room; the lanterns cast a soft glow.

"I am dying, you know," he began, "but if you had not come to the palace, I would have died months ago, and without the pleasure of having known you. It is time to consider how I might care for you in my absence."

Abishag's head bent to the floor so that the king could not see her tears. Would God take him from her too? "I will return to Shunem, my lord. My father's house is still available to me."

The king's fingers squeezed hers lightly. "It burdens me most that you will be alone," he said softly. "Bathsheba told me that Adonijah has asked for you when I am gone."

Abishag's eyes lifted to meet the king's. An unusual defiance sparked in their depths. "I will not belong to Adonijah!"

The king tightened his hand around hers. "No, you will not," he agreed. "The queen also reported Adonijah's behavior toward you. I knew he was attracted to you, but I had no idea he had threatened you in so many ways. I am not sure I will ever forgive him for that."

"I did not ask for his attention, my lord, but I must apologize for being rude to him." Abishag struggled to guard her anger.

"I would never accuse you of flaunting yourself before anyone, child." He paused until Abishag allowed their eyes to meet. "Bathsheba's report confirmed that it was Adonijah who asked for trouble. Fortunately, Rachel was there to protect you. I wish I could have thanked her for that."

For a few minutes, they were silent. Finally, the king took his hand and patted the space next to him on the bed. "Come here, child." Abishag pressed closer to the bed. "Sit here beside me," the king requested.

A wild battle raged within Abishag. How her body longed to be close to the king's, but she dared not believe that her passion could be returned. She was certain the king would not miss the fluttering of her breaths. He would know that she had allowed her heart to love him. It would hurt when he could not reciprocate.

"Please sit down," the king repeated. Abishag silently settled down on the bed next to him. His arm wrapped around her waist. "You are a beautiful woman, Abishag. Any number of men will be begging to care for you."

Abishag tipped her head and refused to look at him. "I do not need any man to care for me."

"But you do need a man to share your passions, child."

"I have no passions."

"Oh, but you do!" the king argued. "Your heart is full of love and laughter just aching to be shared. I can feel it."

"But you cannot choose a man for me," Abishag said.

"Nor can I be that man for you much longer."

There was a sadness in the king's voice that reached deep into Abishag's heart. Her head jerked around to face him. He knew! He understood how her soul longed to unite with his. And he knew as certainly as she did that their time together was limited.

"Lie beside me," he whispered. He tugged at his blankets where she sat. When she stood, he held the blankets up until she had nestled close to him. With her in his arms, he let the blankets fall over her, and they were cocooned in the blankets' warmth.

They said nothing. Abishag closed her eyes so that all her other senses could enjoy their closeness. She smelled the sweet oil she had rubbed into his skin during his morning bath. She heard his soft breaths and felt them on her cheeks. And her belly tingled with unimaginable pleasure feeling his body touching her there. The king's arms held her close. He kissed her forehead.

"I cannot give you my name," he said quietly. "I cannot give you my children. But I can give you the love of an old man who has learned that sometimes friendship is the most precious union two souls can enjoy."

Abishag opened her eyes and looked up into the king's face. He smiled and tugged her closer. Her heart swelled with passion until she could not contain her thoughts silently. "I love you, my lord," she whispered.

"I know," he answered softly. "And I love you."

Darkness settled upon them, and she slept with her heart next to the king's.

Abishag woke late in the night. Her sleepy mind panicked to find herself in the king's bed, but the memory of his invitation calmed her. His breaths were even and deep, and his arm had fallen from around her shoulder. Abishag lay motionless beside him, soaking up the pleasure of their closeness. In the faint light, she could see the outline of his face. How her fingers longed to trace a path from the ridge of his eyebrows, down his nose, across his cheek and past his chin to the softness of his neck. But she forbade her hands to move. Any movement would stir the king, and he might wake to regret her being there. She could not bear the thought.

For hours she lay there. Occasionally the king changed positions, and their bodies had now separated. *It will be better for him if he wakes without me here beside him,* she decided. She lifted the blankets carefully and slipped off the bed. She tucked the blankets close to the king and stood at his bedside. It would be difficult to walk away—to go behind her partitions and climb into her cold bed—but she must. *Surely I only dreamed of lying in the king's arms.*

Abishag slept fitfully until the morning light nudged her awake. Her first thoughts were of the king. How would they greet each other this morning? Had his invitation been offered merely in a moment of pity? Would Bathsheba's visit this morning negate all the affection the king had admitted in the night? How would Abishag bathe him now? Her hands would beg to touch him differently, with a passion she could not disguise any longer. She clung to the security of her bed.

"Abishag?" The king's voice wakened her from another short nap.

"Yes, my lord?"

"Would you . . . help me, please?"

Abishag could barely make out his words from behind her partitions. When she finally made sense of what he had said, she rushed to his bedside.

"I cannot move my arm or my leg," the king whispered when he saw her.

Abishag saw the questions in his eyes. She saw the droop in his right facial muscles. His lips moved awkwardly, as if numb. Her heart raced with fear for his life. She had seen this kind of paralysis before. Sometimes control of the limbs returned, but often it did not. Often, a subsequent attack was fatal.

"Is there pain anywhere?" she asked gently.

The king was barely able to shake his head in response.

No pain. That's good, Abishag assessed. He had been able to speak, and he recognized her, good indications that the attack had not been severe. "Try to move your arm," she encouraged him.

His eyes shut tightly with the effort, but no movement resulted. Abishag slipped her arm behind the king's neck and scooted him to his back. She placed a second pillow behind his head and straightened the blankets over him. She sat on the bed next to him and reached for the hand that he could still control. The passion that had sparked with his touch the night before was subdued now with her concern.

"Can I do anything else to make you comfortable?" she asked. Again, he shook his head. "Shall I send for Bathsheba?" Abishag almost welcomed the queen's company to share her worry for the king's condition.

"She will come." He spoke with effort. "Stay here."

It was all she could do—stay with him and stroke his arm and push the hair back from his face—but it was something. Her mind raced through the herbal concoctions her mother had taught her, but there were none for this kind of attack. She might ease pain with her herbs, but she could not restore control of his limbs. Her helplessness pricked savagely at her heart. She laid her smooth palm against his cheek and caressed his aged skin.

The king struggled to speak. "The harp."

Abishag looked into his eyes and saw another need she could fulfill. She could play music for him and comfort his soul. She scrambled off the bed and started toward her trunk.

"Play mine," the king invited hoarsely.

Abishag returned to the foot of his bed and carefully gathered up his gilded harp. It still seemed a trespass for her to be so bold as to touch the king's harp. Handling the harp was like invading the most private parts of his soul. But he had requested that she play it, and she would rather die than deny him his request.

Abishag settled down on the bed next to the king. As she arranged the harp on her lap and plucked a few introductory chords, she stole a look at him. His eyes were closed and his breaths were steady. Had he not asked her to play, she would have pulled back his blankets and curled up against him, seeking to comfort her own heart more than his. But the queen would be visiting soon. When Bathsheba became aware of the king's condition, his sons would be called as well. Indeed, these very moments might be her last alone with the king.

Her fingers strummed a quiet melody. Though the music was meant to soothe the king, Abishag felt hot tears well up over her eyes and slide down her cheeks. Remembering the consuming effort to mourn silently at her mother's bedside, she tried to brace her shoulders so that they did not shake with her sobs. She swallowed her sorrow in great gulps until she feared she would drown in her own tears. Her heart ached as it vibrated within her chest. She begged her God to take her too if He must take the king.

The doorman knocked before stepping inside with the breakfast tray. It was unlikely that the king would ask for food. Abishag imagined that the very smell of it would turn her own stomach. She remembered the huge platters of food neighbors had delivered to their house in Shunem after her mother's death, and again when her father died. So much food, and the sight of it repulsed her. At times like this, she wanted only to retreat to her soul's cave and wail out her misery. Still, her fingers plucked at the harp's strings. It gave her purpose since all other means of helping were futile.

After a while, the king appeared to have fallen asleep. Abishag slowed the music to an end. She sat very still on the bed. She tried to remember the first day she had stepped into these chambers. There had been an apathetic resignation to her assignment, a sort of hurry to be done with the task so that her life could resume.

But now? What life will I have when the king is gone? Still, begging God to spare his life seemed cruel. There was nothing kingly about being bedfast and needing help with the most basic bodily functions. How could God reward a faithful servant with this kind of gradual death?

"Don't weep." The king's quiet admonition startled her. She felt his fingers touch the back of her arm. "Lie down."

"I should not," Abishag objected. Daylight was beginning to fill the room. The queen would be here soon for her morning visit.

"Please." Even that one word seemed an effort for the king. He was choosing them carefully. His fingers wrapped around her elbow and tugged. "Lie down," he repeated.

It was what Abishag wanted more than anything—to curl up next to him and warm herself with his closeness. And he wanted her there. Not for any kind of physical gratification—that would never happen now—but for the comfort of her touch. She stood and pulled back the blankets. Beside him, she tucked the blankets back into place and slipped her arm beneath them over his chest. Her head found its natural cradle in his shoulder. She stretched out next to him, their bodies touching at every point.

"Thank you," he said when she had settled into place.

"I wish I could do more," Abishag lamented. She moved her hand up to lie against his cheek. What inexpressible comfort she found in touching him.

"This is enough," he replied with effort.

They lay together motionless, as if stirring would destroy the moment. Abishag felt the faint thump of his heartbeats against her own heart. His breaths were sometimes deep and labored and sometimes shallow. The top of her head tingled from the sensation of the air from his nostrils.

In the quiet, Abishag concentrated on awareness of every part of their embrace. It would be hers to relive days from now when she needed the comfort of memories. How could pleasure mingle with such sadness? Yet, it did. Her heart thrilled with the new confirmation that the king returned her affection. At the same time, she ached with the certainty that her time with him was short.

"Thank you," the king whispered a second time.

"For what?"

"For your friendship."

"I would not want to have missed out on knowing you," Abishag replied. "God was good to allow me to be selected to care for you."

"He is good," the king agreed.

Abishag snuggled closer to his side. Emboldened, she pulled her hand under the blankets and smoothed her fingers across his chest. Her hand reached further to his affected arm. She moved her fingertips up and down his skin, hoping to trigger some response. There was none, but the arm he had wrapped around her back squeezed her closer for a moment. Though he could not feel her fingers on his arm, he seemed to understand her hope for a response.

"Please get the queen," he said at last.

Abishag lifted her head to look into his eyes. Struggling to hide her reluctance, Abishag slipped out of the bed and tucked the blankets close to the king. In a language only hearts can understand, their eyes connected and exchanged silent oaths of affection. What an effort it took to turn away from him! Abishag hurried behind her partitions to straighten her robe and push her tangled curls back into place. There was no time for tears now. The king had asked for the queen.

CHAPTER 30

BATHSHEBA SWEPT INTO THE ROOM with Solomon at her side. Abishag could not make her eyes meet theirs. If they were allowed to assess the king's condition for themselves, perhaps it would not seem so critical to them. Perhaps her attachment to the king blurred her objectivity. She moved away from the bedside to allow them closer.

"I am here, my lord," the queen said softly as she lifted the king's hand to her lips. Abishag did not miss the lopped smile that brightened the king's face when Bathsheba spoke to him. "Tell me what I can do for you." Clearly the queen was anxious to comfort the king but uncertain how to do it.

The king shook his head. His hand squeezed around Bathsheba's. Abishag felt anchored to the floor behind them. Her heart begged for comfort for the king, but she wept because it was not she who would provide it.

"Solomon is here," Bathsheba whispered. She loosened her hand from the king's and offered her spot to her son.

"Good morning, Father," Solomon said softly. As if touching might give him strength, the king grasped his son's hand.

"It . . . is time, Son," the king said with labored breaths.

219

Solomon shook his head sadly. "I am ready to be Israel's next king, but I am not ready to tell you goodbye."

"We are fortunate . . . to have this . . . opportunity," the king slurred. He closed his eyes as he spoke. His sighs were long and heavy. Bathsheba dabbed at the saliva that drooled from the king's numbed lips. As long as they were able, the three at the king's bedside would protect his dignity.

"Shall we summon the others?" Solomon asked.

"Not yet," the king answered. "I have . . . those here . . . with me . . . that I want." His body began to shake with chills. Bathsheba turned to direct Abishag to bring more blankets, but she was at the task already. Abishag held the steamed blanket close to her chest until she spread it over the king. She tucked the blankets close around him, but the chills persisted. If only they were alone, she would have stretched out beside him again and shared her body's warmth with him. But they were not alone, and it was the queen who would be preferred.

At last the heat of the blanket choked out the chills, and the king's body settled into a motionless form. "Build . . . the temple, Son. Obey God. Comfort your mother." Like a captain in the army, he issued his final orders carefully. "And protect Abishag."

"You have my word, Father," Solomon assured him.

"Need . . . to rest . . . now," the king said.

Abishag scurried to tend the fire as Bathsheba bent to kiss his cheek. Solomon waited at the door until the queen joined him. Together they waited to talk to Abishag.

"What happened?" Solomon asked her.

"I'm not sure," Abishag answered. "I have seen this before. Sometimes it affects one side of the body, as with the king. Sometimes it affects the whole body."

"Will he improve?" the queen asked.

Abishag knew that they were expecting hopeful words from her. How honest should she be? "It is difficult to tell. If the king's body were not already weakened, his chances to improve would be better."

"So he just lies in bed now, unable to use one half of his body and must speak in slurred and choppy sentences?" Bitterness tinged Solomon's question.

"Most often, the first attack is followed by a second; and that one is likely to involve his whole body—and might take his life." Abishag could barely force the words out of her mouth.

"But sometimes there is improvement?" Solomon probed.

"Sometimes."

"Your father is not reluctant to die, Solomon." Bathsheba had listened quietly to the prognosis Abishag offered. "I would dare say it would not be his wish to tarry in a debilitated way. Wouldn't it be selfish to beg God not to take him yet?"

Age and youth struggled silently. Abishag sympathized with Solomon. Indeed, would she ever be ready to let the king go? Bathsheba, with the perspective gained from a longer and fulfilled life, seemed at peace with the king's imminent death.

Solomon considered his mother's words quietly. "It will happen in God's timing regardless of what we wish. Our choice is to accept it as God's grace in disallowing further suffering or bitterly rebuke God's exercise of His sovereignty by taking Father without our permission."

Bathsheba smiled at her son's words.

Abishag knew it was ridiculous, after all, to think that God might need their permission to do anything. She had found with earlier sorrows that God's grace could enable grieving to be healing and temporary. The king understood that grace. She knew it would comfort him greatly if his loved ones would not argue with God on this point.

Bathsheba appeared to have the same perspective. "Send word immediately if we are needed," she directed Abishag. Then the queen and Solomon slipped out the chamber doors.

Abishag claimed the coveted privacy with the king the moment the door closed behind his son and the queen. She returned to the king's bedside, unshackled from the effort of hiding her affection. He had indeed fallen asleep. Abishag pulled his chair close to sit guard over his comfort. While he slept, there was no evidence of the loss of control of his body. His breathing was relaxed. There were no furrows of pain on his face.

In the silence, Abishag rehearsed their conversation about her future. She had ignored this eventuality far too long, becoming comfortable and burrowed into this appointment to the king. How did one go graciously from the comforts of the palace back to the stark world of common people? Certainly her father's house was still available to her, but she would become a burden to her sister and Joseph if she returned to Shunem. Perhaps what she dreaded most about returning to her village was the constant reminder of what she had sacrificed for Jezreel's future. At this point, there would be none of the security a husband could offer.

The threat of a future with Adonijah put into perspective her fears of returning to Shunem. A shudder of disgust chilled her body when she remembered the touch of that man's hands. There was no erasing from her memory the sneering superiority on his face, as if nothing could be denied him. She *had* denied him, however, and he would not forget. No doubt, the revenge he plotted was intent on ravaging the body she had managed to protect until now. Soon, his visits to these chambers would become more frequent, intent as he would be to seem attentive to his dying father.

Abishag roused from the chair to shake her thoughts of Adonijah. She made her way to the outer chamber to bring the breakfast tray to the king's bedside. She could swallow a few bites while the king rested. Though the food had cooled, she nibbled on a buttered roll. She unfolded the napkin and dabbed at her lips. With the napkin still in her hands, she lifted her glance to find the king watching her.

"Oh!" she whispered. "Can I get something for you to eat?" The king shook his head. "I will ... watch." His words were still slurred, but a faint smile put her at ease. She finished hastily and stacked the meal's dishes on the tray.

"Can I help you with a drink?" Abishag suggested. The king consented with a nod. She poured water into his cup and then slipped her arm behind his neck to raise his head from the pillow. "Drink slowly," she cautioned. "It might be difficult for you to swallow."

The king allowed only a sip. Abishag carefully lowered his head to the pillow and watched his efforts to moisten his lips with his tongue. The lump of flesh moved clumsily and was unsuccessful. Abishag dipped her napkin in her glass and wiped his lips. A heavy sigh from the king betrayed his frustration.

"So helpless," he muttered.

"I am happy to help you," Abishag assured him quickly. She cupped the king's cheek in her palm and rubbed her thumb softly against his skin. "I need to help you as much as you need my help," she confessed. "It would be worse to think that I could do nothing to comfort you."

"Will ... get ... tiresome," the king whispered.

"No, it will not," Abishag argued. He could not imagine how she would treasure the minutes she could spend with him. "Just be patient with me if I don't immediately understand what you need."

Abishag had avoided thoughts of the king becoming unable to speak. Indeed, the time might come when he could not even understand what others were saying to him. It would be the inability to communicate that would make such an existence most unbearable. Abishag prayed that it would not come to that with the king.

"Are you warm enough?" she asked.

"Sometimes," the king replied.

"Are you warm enough now?"

"Do not . . . fret so," he answered wearily. Frustration edged his words.

Abishag turned away at the rebuke.

The king seemed to regret his tone. "Come here," he said. When Abishag faced him, he patted the spot beside him on the bed. "Warm me," he said with a crooked smile.

Abishag settled down without speaking. The king had Solomon for invigorating discussion of his kingdom, his generals for news of his armies, his queen for gentle companionship. And now he had Abishag to warm him. It seemed such an insignificant contribution to his happiness, but it was something she could provide. She stretched out beside him and threw the blankets over her shoulder. Her hand immediately went to his face. Her thumb smoothed across his eyebrow and then rested against the furrowed corners of his eye. Sun and weather had creased the skin. Her soft fingertips could feel the years marked there.

Abishag lay on her side and watched the king in profile. During the months she had cared for him, she had often stolen brief pleasure in watching him. She had become familiar with his body, but it was his face that inspired her affection the most. His eyes were closed as she touched him. When her fingers paused, he turned his head to look at her. A resigned vulnerability looked out from the brown pools. She placed her fingers in the palm of his hand. Like a baby's involuntary movement, the king's fingers closed around hers. For a few moments, their hands bridged their hearts. Words were unnecessary. Silence draped over them like a soft blanket

Abishag nestled closer to the king's side and boldly laid her cheek on his shoulder. She listened to his breaths slow to sleep's pace. Her heart would have held her there forever, but reality marched on in her thoughts. The queen would be returning, and perhaps

Solomon as well. She slipped away from the king's side and tucked the blankets back close to him. She would not allow the palace to belittle her feelings for the king with whispered rumors about her relationship with him. The memory of his spoken affection would be a secret she would guard to her death.

Abishag busied herself at the fireplace, pushing at the hot coals to make room for another log. When she turned back to the king, she found Adonijah's eyes watching her from the chamber doors. A wicked smile slithered across his lips.

"The king is resting," Abishag announced as he approached her.

"I see that," Adonijah replied. "That allows us the opportunity to catch up. I have so missed your visits to my quarters."

"You have no need for nursing," Abishag said. "And there is no other reason why I would be present in your quarters."

"It is a pity I recovered so quickly," he sneered. "The queen reports that my father's health is failing, so you will be busy tending him."

"Tending to the king's needs has always been my commission at the palace," Abishag responded. "I intend to serve him however I can as long as he needs me."

"In hopes that you will be remembered at his death?" he suggested. "You and so many other women who tickled his pleasure occasionally?"

"I have hopes for nothing at his death, but one such as you could not understand that. No doubt there are some who wait impatiently to latch on to what might be left to them." Her accusing eyes defiantly met his.

"Bathsheba will say who gets what." Adonijah nearly spat her name.

"The queen will distribute as the king wished," Abishag replied.

Adonijah snorted at her trust. "You are a fool to expect that."

"As I said, I expect nothing; and I prefer to spend this time comforting the king rather than predicting who might be cheated when he dies."

A faint moan from the king alerted Abishag that he was waking. She turned her back to Adonijah and hurried to the king's bedside.

"Who . . . is here?" the king asked. His eyes remained closed, and speaking took a great effort.

"Adonijah," Abishag answered. "I will give him time alone with you. If you need me, please have him summon me." She slipped past Adonijah and behind the partitions.

"Greetings, Father," Adonijah boomed into the room's silence.

The king forced his eyes open and acknowledged his son's presence.

"You have had a difficult night," Adonijah said.

"I have."

"Perhaps things will improve by tomorrow." Adonijah's tone belittled the king's pain.

"I'm dying," the king said. "Time . . . to settle matters . . . with you."

"Old soldiers live forever," his son quipped.

"Not true," the king said. "I've lived . . . long enough."

Adonijah's silence suggested he finally acknowledged the gravity of his father's condition. Could there be some shred of familial love in his evil heart?

"Solomon will be king," proclaimed the king with a quiet firmness. "You could be an asset to his efforts . . . if you try."

Adonijah laughed. "A humble servant?"

"A supportive brother."

"As you wish," Adonijah mocked.

The king ignored his son's feigned condescension. "Live peacefully . . . together," he urged. He paused to gather his strength. "And . . . do no harm . . . to Abishag."

"What have I to do with that woman?" Adonijah demanded.

"She is . . . not a possession . . . to be tossed about to the highest bidder." The king struggled for each word. "She may remain . . . at the palace . . . if she chooses."

"Would anyone choose to return to Shunem?"

"Her family is there."

"But her fortune is here," came Adonijah's retort.

"The decision . . . is hers. Do not interfere." The command was given quietly but firmly, suggesting consequences for disobedience.

"She is nothing to me," Adonijah professed arrogantly.

"She is . . . precious to *me*. Do her no harm."

Abishag could hear the exchange between the men. Although the king's concern was comforting, it occurred to her that Adonijah might consider it a challenge to be settled at some later time with Solomon. Her situation after the king's death was precarious. She would not give opportunity for either Solomon or Adonijah to determine her future. There was one solution that had been forming in the far corners of her mind. Perhaps it would work out after all.

"I will let you rest now," Adonijah excused himself from the king's bedside. Abishag listened carefully until she heard the chamber doors close behind him. She went to the fireplace and gathered a fresh blanket. She tucked it carefully into place around the king, aware that his eyes followed her movement.

"May I help you with a drink?" she asked when his warmth was ensured.

"I want . . . nothing," the king replied. "Only to sleep."

"It would be good for you to sip a little," Abishag encouraged.

"I cannot," he answered. "Play the harp. That . . . will be good for me."

Abishag returned the untouched cup to the king's tray. She started to fetch her harp from behind the partitions, but the king halted her. "Play mine."

She gathered up the gilded instrument and returned to the bedside. How could she draw music from her heart so devoid of joy? How could her fingers pluck at the strings without loosing the tears that choked her? She simply must, to comfort the king. Her fingers went to the strings, and the room was filled with sweet music.

A faint smile flickered across the king's face. "When you play, I think . . . I am in heaven already."

Abishag smiled down at him. "When you are in heaven, it will be *you* who plays the music you love so much. But for now, I will have to do."

"How many men die without . . . without knowing the pleasure of such music?" he asked.

"How many die without sharing this pleasure with someone they love?" Abishag asked further.

"We are fortunate, you and I," the king agreed. A heavy sigh escaped his lips, and then sleep overtook him.

Abishag kept a silent vigil as he slept.

CHAPTER 31

THE KING ACCEPTED NO MEALS and only a few sips of water throughout the next day. Abishag dabbed his dry lips with a wet cloth. By evening, a pallor had settled across his face. His sleep was restless and brief. Times of wakefulness were consumed with exhausting visits with Solomon and Bathsheba. There seemed to be no end to the king's instructions. He was a true soldier, maintaining watch over his troops even with his last breaths.

Through the following night, Solomon and Bathsheba took turns sitting with Abishag at the king's bedside. Sleep was held at bay only by her dread of missing some small request from the king. The doormen were forewarned to summon the king's family the moment they were alerted. A cloud of death's eventuality settled over the palace. For Abishag, it was a smothering cloud.

Early in the morning, before the sun began to color the horizon, Bathsheba returned to sit with Abishag at the bedside. They whispered, but the king stirred fitfully. Not fully awake, his arms and legs shifted unconsciously as if chasing an elusive comfort. His breaths were deep gasps that filled his chest and then gurgled into the next.

It will not be long, Abishag knew.

The doormen were dispatched. Bathsheba sat tentatively on the edge of the chair at the bedside and gathered up the king's hand into her own. Her lips brushed across his tough skin, and then she held his hand tightly against her cheek.

"I love you, my lord," she whispered.

There was no reply—only the sound of labored breathing that twisted around Abishag's heart until it ached like no time she could ever remember.

Within minutes, the chamber filled with somber family members and ranking officials. Solomon approached his father's bedside with the royal bearing his soldier father would expect of him. He hovered behind Bathsheba protectively, never displacing her from the king's side. Others crowded around the bed and watched helplessly as the queen stroked her fingers through the king's white hair.

Behind them all, Abishag kept a distance from the gathered family, struggling with unworthy desires to be the one at his side stroking his hair. At times, the crowd so pressed around the bed that she could not even see the king's limp form. There was nothing she could do for him now, no comfort to be offered. Her utter uselessness flaunted itself in the face of her sorrowing affection for the king.

She had witnessed enough deaths to know that sometimes there could be a strange rally of strength before the breaths rattled and then just ceased. But sometimes there was simply a quiet slipping from one world to the next.

And so, the king passed.

EPILOGUE

THE MORNING SUN ROSE BEHIND the palace walls and spread its warmth across the busy city. Abishag stood at the door of her home watching a child dig at the earth with a stick. A black mass of tangled curls framed his round little face.

"Mama, look what I have dug up!" he shouted to her excitedly. Abishag went to him and crouched to inspect the dirty rock the boy claimed as his prize. "Will it be a shiny one when I wash it?" he asked.

Abishag watched pudgy fingers wipe away the dirt. "I think it will," she encouraged.

He raised a beaming face from his work. In that instant, she caught a glimpse of King David's deep-brown eyes set in the freckled face of this child. There had been moments of breathtaking resemblance like this before, and not without reason. This child, Abishag's child, was the son of Joshua, the son of Rachel, the king's concubine. He was the rainbow God had sent to remind her of the days when she had comforted a king.